THE SPANISH KIDNAPPING DISASTER

MARY DOWNING HAHN is the author of more than a dozen books for young people including the award winning *Stepping on the Cracks*. She is a former children's librarian who lives in Columbia, Maryland, with her husband, Norm.

THE SPANISH KIDNAPPING DISASTER

MARY DOWNING HAHN

AN AVON CAMELOT BOOK

AVON BOOKS
A division of
The Hearst Corporation
1350 Avenue of the Americas
New York, New York 10019

First Avon Camelot Printing: April 1993

Printed in the U.S.A.

OPM   10   9   8   7   6   5   4

For my friends at the
International School of Stuttgart
and
The American School of Madrid

Without your help and companionship
this book could not have been written!

THE SPANISH KIDNAPPING DISASTER

Although we didn't know it then, our troubles began when Amy lost her barrette. It was one of a pair decorated with cloisonné butterflies, and, if we'd been able to see into the future, neither one of us would have turned back to look for it.

We were in Toledo, Spain, at the time, but, because of the situation, we weren't having much fun. You see, my mother had just married Amy's father, a union we had both opposed, and now, due to circumstances beyond everybody's control, Amy, her little brother, Phillip, and I were tagging along on the honeymoon. No one, including Mom and Don, was enjoying our first experience as a family.

Don't ask me why I agreed to help Amy search the gutters of Toledo for something less than two inches long. I certainly didn't care whether her hair fell in her eyes or not. Combed or uncombed, washed or unwashed, it always looked better than mine. What's more, I didn't like Amy, and she didn't like me. I think I went with her because I was tired of walking behind Mom, ignored and forgotten while she held hands with Don. I was definitely fed up with Phillip, one of the most irritating ten-year-olds I'd ever met.

Anyway, it was late afternoon, and Amy and I had been dragging along behind the others, too hot and tired to walk faster or even quarrel. Several feet ahead, Phillip was practicing his Spanish on every innocent bystander he saw. Mom was reading loudly from her guidebook, unaware that nobody was listening. And Don was photographing alleys, stairways, people, cats, dogs, pigeons — ordinary things tourists never noticed but which he felt represented the real Spain. No one was paying any attention to Amy or me. I suppose our parents thought two twelve-year-old girls could take care of themselves.

Then Amy noticed her barrette was gone, and, while Phillip, Mom, and Don strolled on, we walked off in the opposite direction to look for it. While Amy peered into every crack and crevice big enough to hide the barrette, I paused to take a picture of some brightly colored laundry hanging on a sunny balcony. Suddenly, a crowd of tourists in black business suits filled the street and began photographing the laundry too. There were so many of them Amy and I couldn't see past them or even wiggle around them. By the time they'd put their cameras away and moved on to the next attraction, we didn't see Mom, Don, or Phillip anywhere.

The barrette forgotten, we looked at each other. "Where did they go?" Amy asked.

Hoping to catch up with our parents, we ran to the corner, but all we saw were the backs of the tourists disappearing around a turn in the street.

"Mom said something about the Alcázar," I said. "We'll just ask somebody how to get there. It's such a big old building, I bet everyone knows where it is."

"But we're in Spain," Amy reminded me. "Suppose we can't find anyone who speaks English?"

"No problem," I said with more confidence than I felt. "I have a great sense of direction."

From the way Amy looked at me, I knew she had no faith in me or my sense of direction. Probably she was remembering the time I'd shown her a shortcut to the mall, and we'd ended up lost in a swamp. She'd ruined her favorite sandals, fallen into a patch of poison ivy, and been bitten by three million mosquitos before we found our way to dry ground. Amy's not the kind of person who forgets a thing like that, especially if she thinks you did it on purpose.

"Tell the truth for once," she said crossly. "You don't have the slightest idea where the Alcázar is and you know it."

"Don't get mad and blame this on me," I said. "You're the one who lost the barrette. I was just trying to help you find it."

Making an attempt to stay calm, I looked at the silent buildings and the empty streets, but they offered no clues to the Alcázar's whereabouts. It could have been uphill or down, east, west, north, or south. And there was no one to ask. A white cat regarded me solemnly from a balcony. A dog wandered past, sniffing the curb. A flock of pigeons flew up into the air with a clatter of wings. But not a single person appeared. All the doors were closed, and the windows were shuttered against the hot June sun.

"What should we do?" Amy asked, suddenly tearful.

Not wanting to admit I was just as scared as she was, I took a wild guess and pointed down the street. "It's that way."

"Are you sure?" Amy asked suspiciously.

Without answering, I walked off as if I knew exactly where I was going, and Amy followed me. After trudging along in silence for about five minutes, we turned a corner and saw a sunlit square. A number of streets curved out of it, but there was no sign of the Alcázar.

"Now what, Miss Know It All?" Amy glared at me. Without the barrette, her hair tumbled down over one eye, and she brushed it back from her face impatiently. Half moons darkened the armpits of her blue tee-shirt, and she looked as hot and cross as I felt.

Across the square, a woman sat on the curb adjusting her sandal strap. A shabby backpack leaned against the wall behind her. Although she was wearing faded jeans and a tee-shirt, the flower in her long red hair gave her a foreign look.

"Maybe she can help us," I said.

"I bet she won't understand a thing you say," Amy muttered, but she crossed the square with me.

I stopped in front of the woman. When she didn't look up, I cleared my throat nervously. "Excuse me," I said, "do you speak English?"

The woman smiled. "I have a little English," she said,

forming each word slowly and carefully. "You are lost?"

Fascinated by her accent, I stared at her, momentarily speechless. She wore big gold hoops in her ears, and she was beautiful in a way Amy, pretty as she was, would never be. Tall and slender, the woman reminded me of a model I'd seen once on the cover of *Vogue*. She had the same high cheekbones, big eyes, and square chin. Except for a sprinkle of freckles bridging her nose, her skin had been bronzed by the sun to a smooth rosy gold.

"We got separated from our parents," Amy said, "and now we can't find them." She frowned as if she didn't expect much help from a person who couldn't speak perfect English, and her eyes brimmed with tears.

"They were on their way to the Alcázar." My voice came back in a rush as I tried to make up for Amy's unfriendliness. "Can you tell us how to get there?"

The woman rose and hoisted her backback onto her shoulders. It was very heavy from the look of it. "I go toward the Alcázar myself. I will take you," she said. "Girls of your age should not be alone in the streets. There is danger. Many thieves, pickpockets. You must be careful with whom you speak."

Amy looked at me as if her every fear had just been vocalized. Then she scrutinized the woman's face and clothes as if she weren't sure she should speak to her, let alone accompany her through the streets of Toledo.

"Don't just stand there," I said to Amy as the woman began to walk away. "You heard what she said. She'll take us to the Alcázar."

Amy sighed and shoved her hair behind her ears. "I hope so," she muttered, but, to my satisfaction, she followed me down the narrow street our guide had taken.

What choice did either one of us have? There was no one else to ask, no one else to follow.

2

eaving Amy behind, I caught up with the woman. "My name is Felix," I said. "What's yours?"

"Felix?" She stared at me. "Never have I met a girl called Felix. That is most unusual, even in America, is it not?"

"My real name is Felicia," I admitted, "but nobody calls me that except my mother when she's mad at me."

"Well, then, Felix, I am glad to meet you." The woman offered me her hand and I shook it.

"I am Grace," she went on, "and I am a traveler here in *España*. That is not the same as a *turista*, you know. Unlike most strangers in this beautiful country, I am in love with Spain. The sun, the golden light it gives, the old stone that glows. It is in my soul, *mi alma*." Grace struck her chest forcibly with her fist. "You understand?"

"Oh, yes," I said. "I adore Spain too." To prove it, I thumped my chest so hard it hurt.

Grace smiled at me and then looked at Amy. If she expected a similar display of passion from her, she was disappointed. Amy was paying no attention to Grace and me. From the way she was staring at buildings and street names, you would think we were still lost.

"Are you sisters?" Grace asked me.

"No!" I said quickly. "My mother just married her father. This is their honeymoon."

"They have brought you with them?" Grace sounded surprised.

"Well, they didn't mean to. We were supposed to stay with Amy's grandmother, but she fell and broke her hip just before the wedding, so here we are."

"You must be very rich to take such a trip together," Grace said.

"Not really," I said, trying to be modest and truthful, two qualities which did not come easily to me.

"Oh, please, I know better. All Americans are rich," Grace said. "They say they are not, but in your country the poorest one is richer than most in my country. I think you all live like the television shows I see. *Dallas, Dynasty, Falcon Crest.* You are fortunate, Felix, very, very fortunate."

Grace's eyes narrowed a little, and, for a second, I was afraid she had taken a sudden dislike to me. Then she smiled, and I felt better again. She'd sized me up, I thought, and decided I was okay after all.

"Tell me about yourself," she said. "Where do you live? What is your home like? Is it big like the ones on television?"

"We just bought a new house," I began truthfully enough, "in Woodhaven Estates. It's got a big yard, and five bedrooms. Very expensive. You should see my room.

The walls are pale lavender, and I have a canopy bed with lots of pillows and wall-to-wall carpeting. I have my own TV too, one of those big screens built into the wall so it's almost like being at the movies."

When I paused for breath, I noticed Amy was staring at me. She was probably jealous because Grace was paying attention to me instead of her. Amy's used to being the star attraction.

Or was it because I was beginning to exaggerate? It wasn't quite true what I'd said about my room. I did have a canopy bed, bought cheap at a yard sale, but my TV was an old black and white portable that only picked up three channels. And there was so much junk on the floor most of the time you couldn't even see the carpet.

Ignoring Amy, I smiled at Grace and moved into a higher gear of exaggeration, one that came pretty close to lying. "My real father," I said, "gives me everything I want. When I go home, he's going to buy me a horse."

"Ah," said Grace. "Your own horse, Felix, how lovely."

"Yes, a purebred Arabian, I think." I didn't dare look at Amy for fear she would tell Grace there was no way my father would ever buy me a horse. He had about as much interest in me as you might have in a pair of shoes you'd outgrown. Mom was lucky to get a child support check from him once or twice a year, especially since he'd remarried and started a new family. I once heard her tell someone I was his practice kid. But why tell Grace the truth?

Basking in her attention, I chattered on and on about Mom's Volvo and Don's Porsche. To keep the conversation going, I threw in descriptions of the Jacuzzi and the swimming pool we'd be getting soon, the country club we'd be joining, and the private school I might attend in the fall. I actually told Grace my mother had a mink coat even though she belongs to Greenpeace and hates women who wear fur.

And what was Amy doing while I let my tongue run away with my brain? She was stalking along behind us, her mouth shut as tight as the lid on a new peanut butter jar. I knew she was mad, but I couldn't stop talking. The more Grace believed, the more I lied.

Later, of course, I realized I'd made a big mistake. But it was partly Amy's fault. Instead of sighing and shaking her head, she should have told Grace the Volvo was twelve years old and in need of major repairs, she should have told her the Porsche burned oil and spent most of its time in the shop. She should also have said there were no Jacuzzis, private schools, fur coats, country clubs, or horses in our future.

But did she? No indeed. Amy let me blab on and on, and she didn't even try to stop me. Not once.

3

After a long, hot walk up and down hills and in and out of little squares, we came to the cathedral. Wiping the sweat from her forehead, Grace leaned against a wall and shrugged her backpack from her shoulders.

"Ah," she sighed, "that's better. It gets so hot and heavy sometimes."

Just as I was making myself comfortable in a shady place, Amy turned to Grace. "Are you sure you know where the Alcázar is? It seems to me we should've gotten there a long time ago."

"Do not worry, it is not far now," Grace said. "I must rest for a while. Be patient, please." Ignoring Amy's restlessness, Grace bent down to examine the strap of her sandal again. The leather was frayed, and she was having trouble keeping it buckled.

In the sunny square, a few feet away, a man stood in front of an easel. He was painting a picture of the cathedral. Ignoring Grace and me, Amy watched him silently. Her face was as expressionless as the stone angels peering down at us from the walls, but I knew she was angry.

Sooner or later, I was going to hear about this episode. Like our adventure in the swamp, Amy would add being lost in Toledo to her list of grievances.

Well, it was too late to worry about Amy. Besides I wanted to learn more about Grace. "Now that I've told you all about me," I said, "what about you?"

Grace shrugged. "Me? There is nothing to tell, Felix."

"Oh, there must be." I gazed at her, soaking up the aura of mystery that surrounded her. "For instance," I persisted, "where are you from?"

"It is not important," Grace said. "I am a wanderer, a nomad. I left my home behind many years ago."

"Are you Spanish?"

"No." Grace smiled as if she were playing Twenty Questions with me.

"Well, what then?" I asked, annoyed to be treated like an ignorant child. "Are you French? German? Russian?"

Grace tossed her hair, and her earrings swayed against her cheeks. "Call me a citizen of the world, if you must, someone from everywhere and nowhere."

I paused a moment to catch my breath and think about that — a citizen of the world. It sounded so exotic, so free, so sophisticated. Gazing up at the cathedral's spires, I decided I too would be a person from everywhere and nowhere. As soon as I graduated from high school, I would cram my belongings into a backpack, fasten a flower in my hair, and leave home forever.

"You must live somewhere." Amy's dry, practical voice interrupted my fantasy of myself as a woman with haunted eyes, leaving a string of broken-hearted men behind me as I roamed the beaches of Portugal or climbed the mountains of Tibet, always alone, shadowed by past tragedies.

"I made homes in many places," Grace told Amy. "Egypt, Israel, Turkey, here in *España.*"

Amy was obviously not impressed by Grace's answer. Looking at her watch, she frowned. "Fascinating as this is, I wish you'd either take us to the Alcázar or tell us how to get there. My father must be worried to death about me."

From the way Amy spoke you would think Don and Don alone cared where we were. My mother was probably worried too — that is, if she'd noticed my absence. The way she acted around Don, holding his hand, kissing him, clinging to him, she might have forgotten she had a daughter by now.

"Forgive me," Grace said to Amy. "I would not want to worry your father." Hoisting her backpack into place, she set off across the square.

"You are so rude," I whispered to Amy. "Can't you see how tired she is?"

"At least I'm not dumb enough to be taken in by all that citizen of the world stuff," Amy said. "She's probably a bigger liar than you. If that's possible."

Hoping Grace hadn't heard Amy, I hurried after her. She was halfway up a narrow flight of stairs, a shortcut to the street above. The houses on either side were so close you could stretch out your arms and touch them, and the steps were worn down in the middle by the feet of all the thousands of people who had climbed them. Like every-thing in Toledo, they were old and romantic and mys-terious.

At the top, Grace paused to readjust her backpack. We had reached a narrow street, partly shaded by tall build-ings. The sunlight slanted down a wall, glinting on Grace's hair and etching tiny lines around her eyes.

"Where do you go next, Felix?" she asked. "After you leave Toledo?"

"Tomorow we're driving to Segovia," I told her, "and after that Ávila."

Grace smiled. "Ah, the castle in Segovia is the loveliest in Spain, and you will see windmills on the way to Ávila. Old ones on the hilltops, the very same that Don Quixote mistook for his enemies."

"Right now all I want to see is the Alcázar," Amy said.

Ignoring Amy's bad manners, Grace took her arm and said, "Look, there it is." She pointed at a sunlit square opening out of the shadows at the end of the street. At one end was the Alcázar, towering over the shops huddling at its feet.

"I see Daddy!" Without even thanking Grace, Amy broke away and ran toward Don.

"That is your mother? The blonde woman?" Grace stared with some interest at Mom as she hurried toward us.

"Would you like to meet her? I'm sure she'll be very grateful to you for bringing me back." I grabbed Grace's hand, thinking how impressed Mom would be to meet a citizen of the world.

But Grace shook her head. "No, not now, Felix," she said. "I have an appointment and I am already late."

"Wait," I cried as she turned away. "Will I ever see you again?"

Grace paused and looked over her shoulder at me. "Perhaps," she called. "One never knows what fate holds."

"Come back!" I tried to run after her, but a gang of teenagers burst out of an alleyway and surged between us. Standing on tiptoe, I searched for Grace, but all I saw was a flash of red hair in the sunlight. Then she was gone, and I was alone in a crowd of tourists pointing their cameras at everything.

4

As I tried to push my way past a man wielding a huge video camera, I felt someone seize my shoulder.

"Felix," Mom cried. She threw her arms around me and hugged me so hard I thought my ribs would crack. "Where have you been? I've been so worried!"

"We got lost." For a moment I snuggled close, enjoying the attention and the feel of her arms around me. Then I remembered Grace. Pulling back from Mom, I searched for a glimpse of red hair in the crowd. "The nicest woman brought us here. I wanted you to meet her."

"But the Alcázar is less than a five-minute walk from where we left you," Mom said, "and you've been gone almost fifteen minutes. What took you so long?"

"Amy and I must have walked the wrong way before we met Grace," I said. "But she was wonderful, Mom, and really beautiful too. She said she was a citizen of the world. Can you imagine?"

I looked at Mom, expecting to see her eyes light with pleasure, but she wasn't really listening to me. All she said was, "Thank goodness, you're safe. We were just about to go to the police. Don't ever disappear like that again!"

The anger in her voice upset me, and I shrugged her arm away from my shoulder. "I'm surprised you noticed I was gone."

Mom stared at me. "What are you talking about?"

"We've been in Spain a week," I said, "and you've hardly looked at me once. The only person you see is Don, Don, Don."

"Felicia," Mom said, "how can you say such a thing?"

"It's true," I said. "Now that you have him, you don't care about me anymore."

"Don't be silly." Mom tried to hug me but I wouldn't let her.

Then Don joined us, and Mom forgot all about me. Letting him take her hand, she strolled toward the shops in the square. With Phillip and Amy, I was left to trail along behind.

"It's about time you all showed up." Phillip scowled at Amy and me. "Dad wouldn't even let me look at swords, he was so worried about you. You'd think somebody had kidnapped you or something the way he was carrying on. I told him nobody would want either one of you, but that just made him get mad at me."

"Oh, poor little Phillip," Amy said, "I'm so sorry I inconvenienced you."

Her voice dripped with sarcasm but Phillip didn't notice. He'd spotted some swords in a shop window and was rapidly scanning his Spanish phrase book, searching, no doubt, for a new way to embarrass us.

Ever since we'd arrived at the Madrid Airport, Phillip

had been trying to speak Spanish. So far, no one had understood a word he said. His efforts only confused people and made everything take two or three times longer than it should have. Any normal person would have been discouraged, but not Phillip. He kept right on trying, speaking louder and louder as if he thought the poor Spaniards were deaf.

"Can we go in here?" Phillip grabbed Don's arm and tugged him toward the swords. "You said you'd buy me a sword as soon as we found Amy and Felix. Come on, Dad, please?"

As Phillip's voice rose like the sound of a mosquito on a hot day, I winced. "Stop whining," I told him. "It hurts my ears."

"I'm not whining," Phillip shrilled.

"You are so," Amy said, surprising me. Usually she'd rather die than agree with me. For instance, if I said it was a nice day, she would say it was about to rain, even if the sun was shining. But she was obviously as tired of hearing Phillip's voice as I was.

"You shut up, you *pulpo*," Phillip said.

"Dad, he's swearing at me in Spanish." Amy pushed herself in between Mom and Don. "Make him stop."

Phillip grinned at Don. "I only called her a *pulpo*," he said. "It means 'octopus.' "

As Don turned from Amy to Phillip and back again, Mom seized his hand. "Look, Don, what beautiful jewelry." Skillfully she diverted everyone's attention to a display of earrings next to the swords Phillip had been admiring. "Shall we go inside and see them?"

All five of us crowded into the store. While Phillip led Don to a rack of swords, Mom and Amy stopped to admire a display of china figurines. Leaving them, I went in search of earrings. To my delight, I found some gold hoops as big as Grace's. Although Mom tried to persuade me to buy a pair of silver butterflies like the ones Amy chose, I held out for the hoops.

As soon as my new earrings were paid for, I removed the little stars I usually wore and put them on. The hoops hung almost to my shoulders, and I thought they made me look worldly and slightly mysterious. All I needed was a flower in my hair.

When we had all bought what we wanted, we walked slowly down the hill toward our hotel. At the Plaza de Zocodover, a big square full of sidewalk cafes, Mom and Don decided to rest for a while. Amy and Phillip ordered sodas, but I followed Mom's example and asked for *café con leche*. It turned out to be coffee foaming with steamed milk, quite bitter, and I sipped it slowly, feeling sophisticated.

Amy's giggle interrupted my daydream. "What's the big joke?" I glared at her over the rim of my cup.

"Those earrings," she said. "They look so funny."

I tried to ignore her, but my vision of myself slipped sidewise and I saw what Amy saw. A tall, gawky girl with freckles, crooked teeth, and shaggy brown hair wearing a red tee-shirt with a cow on it, a gift from Aunt Martha in Vermont. Amy was right. I shouldn't have bought the earrings. No matter how beautiful they were, they couldn't make me into a citizen of the world. Unlike Grace, I wasn't the right type to wear big gold hoops in my ears.

As I slid down in my seat, too embarrassed to look at anyone, I felt Mom pat my knee. "I love your earrings," she whispered. "In fact, I might even go back and get a pair for myself."

I leaned toward her. "You don't think they look dumb?" I asked, keeping my voice low so Amy wouldn't hear.

"Not at all," Mom said. Then she pulled out her camera and took a picture of me which Phillip almost ruined by waving his sword in front of her just as she pressed the shutter.

"How about me?" he asked. "Don't I make a good matador?"

While Phillip posed for a picture, Amy turned to me. "See that guy?" She directed my attention to a man wearing a black leather jacket sitting at a table several yards away. "He's been staring at me ever since we got here. I bet he thinks I'm older."

"Don't kid yourself," I said. "He's probably looking at her." I pointed at a girl perched on a wall behind us. She was wearing a short leather skirt and a lot of make-up. Her boyfriend sat next to her, whispering in her ear and making her laugh.

Annoyed, Amy tossed her head and managed to swat me with her hair. The cobwebby feel of it tickled my nose, and I moved closer to Mom. I was hoping for a little more of her attention, but she was too engrossed in something Don was saying to notice me. Feeling neglected, I sipped my *café con leche* and stole another look at the man in the black leather jacket. He was staring at our table all right, but not at Amy. At the moment his eyes were fixed on Don.

When his gaze suddenly shifted to me, I lowered my head, hoping he hadn't noticed I'd been watching him watching us. Maybe it was the black jacket, maybe it was the mustache hiding the corners of his mouth, maybe it was the dark hair slanting down over his eyes, maybe it was just the way he sat there all by himself staring at us, but something about him made me very uncomfortable.

I turned to Mom, but just as I was about to tell her about the man, Don hugged her and she kissed him. No matter what I said now, she wouldn't be interested. Not with Don whispering in her ear.

"Can't that stuff wait till we get to the hotel, Dad?" Phillip asked as Don kissed Mom.

"Kids," Don said to Mom, laughing. "Sometimes they act like stuffy old adults, don't they?"

Mom nodded. "We should go anyway," she said. "We have a dinner reservation at eight-thirty."

Reluctant to leave, I lagged behind the others. The moon was just coming out, and the tables were filling with people. Thinking Grace might be here somewhere, sipping *café con leche* too, I scanned the crowd for her red hair. That was when I noticed that the man in the black leather jacket was still watching us. Worse, he'd been joined by another man, older and kind of heavyset. They were sitting side by side talking, but it was Mom and Don they were looking at.

Then the older man saw me. For a second, we stared at each other across the crowded square. It was like locking eyes with a cobra. Paralyzed with fear, I couldn't move or look away. When the man turned his head, I hurried after Mom and seized her hand.

"What's wrong, Felix?" she asked. "Did something scare you?" She was smiling, but she sounded concerned. It wasn't often I held her hand.

"There was a man. He was staring at me." I looked back at the square, but the table where the two men had been sitting was empty. "He's gone," I said. "But there were two of them. One watched us the whole time we were having our coffee. Then the other came."

"Oh, Felix, you and your imagination." Mom smiled at me as if I were five years old and squeezed my hand. "Maybe he was admiring your earrings. Or your tee-shirt. Maybe he wanted one just like it, cow and all."

"Don't treat me like a dumb little kid," I said, but she was already walking away, eager to catch up with Don. Why did she blame all my worst fears on my imagination? It wasn't fair. Some things were real. I hadn't dreamed up the look in that man's eyes.

Suddenly afraid to be alone, I rushed after Mom. Slipping my hand into hers again, I glanced back at the square, but it had lost all its charm. In the dusk, it looked sinister and full of danger. Somewhere in the crowd was a man with cobra eyes, a man I didn't want to see again.

5

After dinner, we went straight to our rooms. "We're getting an early start tomorrow," Don reminded the three of us before he disappeared with Mom. "Get a good night's sleep, all right?"

As soon as he left, Amy drew a line with her finger down the middle of the double bed. "This is my side," she told me, gesturing to make it perfectly clear.

"Don't worry," I said. "I have no intention of encroaching on your space."

"My, what big words you know," Amy said sarcastically. "You must have eaten your talented and gifted vocabulary lists."

When Phillip laughed, Amy was encouraged to add, "You were probably starving. Anything would taste better than the food your mother fixes."

Without hesitating, I decided to escalate the war of insults. Amy had been criticizing Mom's meals since she'd eaten her first dinner with us, way back when neither one of us suspected that we'd be sisters someday. I was tired of listening to her.

"My mother may not be a gourmet cook," I said, "but

she's home every night. *She* didn't run away with her music appreciation teacher."

This was a low blow, aimed at Amy's mother, the former Mrs. Capshaw, who had indeed eloped with a professor from the community college. But Amy had asked for it. My mother had spent four years in college learning to be a chemist in a laboratory, not a slave in a kitchen.

For a moment Amy and Phillip stared at me as if my words had turned them to stone. Then Amy's face flushed scarlet. "Well," she said, "at least my mother sees Phillip and me every Sunday. She doesn't just mail a check two or three times a year like your father!"

For emphasis, Amy hurled one of her fashion magazines at me. I ducked, and it whacked the wall behind me.

"You shut up!" I yelled. "My dad sees me whenever he can! He can't help it if he has to travel all over the world!" Furious, I threw the magazine back at Amy, but I was too mad to aim well. It sailed wide of its target and knocked a lamp off the dresser instead of hitting her.

"I'm telling," Phillip squealed and ran for the door.

"Tattletale," I shouted as the door opened and Don appeared with Mom behind him.

"Hold it," Don said. "Can't we leave you kids alone for five minutes without a fight starting?"

"Amy said you were a bad cook," I told Mom.

"Felix insulted my mother," Amy told Don.

"They were both yelling," Phillip chimed in, "and Felix threw a magazine and knocked over the lamp, but I didn't do anything. I was just trying to go to sleep."

"She started it," Amy and I said together as if we'd practiced.

"Well, you can both stop," Mom said as Don picked up the lamp and set it on the bureau. "Right now." She frowned equally at both Amy and me to show how fair she was being. "Tell Amy you're sorry, Felix."

"And you apologize to Felix," Don told Amy.

"I'm not sorry," I said to Mom. "She's a stuck-up, conceited brat."

"I'm not sorry either." Amy glared at me. "She's a loud-mouthed showoff, and I hate her!"

Mom and Don looked at each other. In the silence, Phillip said, "Can we go to bed now? I'm sleepy."

"Not until I hear some apologies." Don folded his arms across his chest and stared hard, first at Amy, then at me.

"Come on, you all," Phillip begged. "Just say it. Who cares if you mean it?"

As Don turned to Phillip, Amy and I exchanged nasty looks. At the same time, Mom gave me a little nudge toward Amy. "Be a good sport, Felix," she said.

"Okay, okay," I mumbled, shrinking away from Mom's hand. "I'm sorry, Amy." Silently I added, "Sorry the magazine hit the lamp instead of you, sorry I have to say this, sorry I'm in Spain with you, and, most of all, sorry my mother married your father."

Then Amy muttered her apologies, probably adding a few silent qualifications herself, and Don and Mom smiled at us in a benign, parental way.

"Now can we go to sleep?" Phillip asked.

"That's a wonderful idea," Don said. He yawned and winked at Mom.

"No more fighting, kids — okay?" Mom lingered a moment, her hand on the doorknob. "We're a family now. Let's act like one."

As soon as the light went out, Phillip flopped down on his rollaway bed. From where I lay next to Amy, I could hear the tinny sound of his Walkman, and I knew he was listening to his "Spanish for Travelers" tape. Ever since we'd boarded the plane in Baltimore, he had played it over and over again — even when he was asleep. He claimed the words went straight from his ears into his brain and lodged there. Next year when he was in sixth grade, he planned to prove it for his science fair project.

I tried to fall asleep, but I was intensely aware of Amy on the other side of her imaginary line. I didn't want any part of me to touch any part of her. Every time I moved, I worried about poking her, but I couldn't lie still. My legs were twitchy and so were my feet. To make it worse, I kept seeing the man with the cobra eyes. Why couldn't I forget him?

After I'd rolled from my side to my back to my stomach several times, Amy sat up. "What's the matter with you?" she asked. "Are you hyper or something?"

"I can't sleep," I said.

"You and I followed that weird woman all over Toledo and you're not tired?" Amy stared at me. "I'm exhausted, so if you don't mind, if it's not too much trouble, lie still and let me sleep!"

"Grace isn't weird," I said. "Honestly, Amy, how can

you be so ungrateful? She rescued us from being lost, didn't she?"

"You never even noticed we passed the same square two or three times, did you?" Amy asked. "You were too busy lying about horses and swimming pools and Jacuzzis!"

"I was just —"

"Showing off." Amy completed my sentence for me. "Like you always do. You wanted her to think we were millionaires or something."

"I did not —"

"You're a liar, Felix, admit it." Amy was really mad now. "I was embarrassed half to death!"

As I bit my lip, trying to think of a good comeback, Phillip suddenly yelled, "If you *estúpidos pulpos* don't shut up, I'm telling!"

"You hush," Amy shouted at him, "and you too, Felix!" Then she flopped down with her back to me. She huffed a couple of times, but she didn't say another word.

I lay beside her, staring at the shadows on the ceiling and thinking about what she'd just said. Grace had taken us past the same square more than once? How could I have failed to notice that? Amy must be mistaken. After all, one square looked pretty much the same as another. She was probably confused. And what reason would Grace have to lead us in circles? It didn't make sense.

Shutting my eyes tightly, I told myself I was going to forget about everything and go to sleep. But then I remembered the man at the Plaza de Zocodover, the one who had scared me. With his face in front of me again, I couldn't relax.

"Amy," I whispered, "are you asleep?"

"What do you want now?" Amy asked, keeping her back to me. Her voice sounded as if she were forcing it out between clenched teeth.

"Do you remember that man in the black leather jacket?"

"He was really handsome, wasn't he?" Amy turned over then and looked at me. "He reminded me of a movie star."

"Did you see the other man?"

She frowned. "What other man? He was all by himself."

"No," I said, "Another man came and sat down with him. He was older, heavier. Meaner."

"Meaner?" Amy stared at me.

I nodded. "His eyes were scary," I said. "And they were both staring at us, *all* of us. Not just you."

Amy sighed. "Do you know what's wrong with you, Felix? You have too much imagination. At least that's what my father thinks."

I shook my head. "Mom says the same thing, but I didn't imagine that man and I didn't imagine the way he was looking at us. He scared me."

"Listen, Felix," Amy said. "I want to go to sleep, okay? I don't want to hear about mean men with scary eyes or anything else. Can't you just lie still like a normal person and be quiet?"

Her voice was rising again, and Phillip made a funny snuffling sound right in the middle of a snore. Not wanting him to wake up, I lay down on my back and told myself I would not move or speak till morning. I would not think of the man again, I would not worry about him, I would lie still like a normal person and not bother anyone.

Pretty soon, Amy fell asleep. Lying so close, I could hear her breathing. Although she didn't snuffle and snort like Phillip, I couldn't forget she was there, right beside me.

As quietly as possible I rolled over a couple of times, trying to find a comfortable position, but I couldn't stop thinking. My brain just wouldn't turn off. When I banished the man from my thoughts, Grace popped up and took his place. I saw her face again, her gold earrings, her long red hair. If only I could grow up to be like her, free and beautiful, a citizen of the world.

Now that it was too late, I was sorry I had lied to her. It didn't help to remind myself I'd probably never see her again. I just couldn't stop feeling bad about all the crazy ideas I'd given her. No wonder Amy didn't like me. I really was a dope sometimes.

6

The next morning, after a lot of misunderstandings and confusion about breakfast, checking out, and loading the car, we finally got under way around nine o'clock. Since none of us seemed improved by our night's sleep or our morning activities, Don put "La Bamba" in the tape deck, turned it up as loud as he could, and drove out of Toledo.

While he and Mom sang along with the music, I pressed my face against the window and watched the tile roofs, the cathedral, and the Alcázar gradually shrink and disappear into the distance like a dream of a city.

"Someday I'll come back," I thought. "I'll drink *café con leche* in the Plaza de Zocodover and watch the lights come on in the city. I'll have my own little house with a balcony and a cat to keep me company. And I'll wear a flower in my hair. A citizen of the world, that's what I'll be."

Leaning back in my seat, I touched my earrings and tried to picture my grown-up self, but it was Grace's face I saw, not mine. As the scenery flashed by, brown fields,

30 ·

bulls, olive groves, little towns with balconied apartment houses, I wondered where she was and if I would ever see her again.

·

The castle in Segovia more than lived up to Grace's description. It was so beautiful it hardly seemed to belong in the real world. Like a palace in fairyland, its walls glowed against a cloudless blue sky. On the towers high overhead, the yellow and red Spanish flag fluttered in the breeze.

After going through the usual confusion of buying tickets, aggravated by Phillip's misguided attempts to translate, we went inside. While Mom read us passages from her guidebook describing the Moorish influence on the castle's architecture, we wandered from room to room until we found a spiral staircase leading to the highest tower. The steps were steep and narrow. People were pushing their way down as we climbed up, and I had to fight to reach the top without being shoved down the stairs. When I finally stepped out into the sunlight, though, the view was worth every inch of the climb.

Wandering away from the others, I leaned over the parapet and gazed at the distant mountains. Far below me, a hawk floated on the breeze, its wings spread like fingertips.

As I watched the hawk dip and glide, I heard Phillip say, "That's her?"

Turning around, I saw him and Amy staring at someone standing beside Mom on the opposite side of the tower.

Although the woman's back was to me, her red hair was unmistakable.

"What's Grace doing talking to your mother?" Amy asked me.

"How should I know?" Anxiously I shoved through the crowd of tourists separating me from Mom and Grace. A woman frowned at me when I stepped on her toe, but I was too worried to apologize. I had to reach Mom before anything was said about horses, swimming pools, or Jacuzzis.

Pushing my hair behind my ears to show off my hoops, I slid in between Mom and Grace.

"You're right," Mom was saying to Grace. "I've never seen such a beautiful view."

Don smiled and nodded, but he was too busy taking pictures to talk.

Mom was the first to notice me. "This nice woman has been telling me about the castle, Felix, and the things you can see from here," she said. "For instance, those little specks on the horizon way over there are windmills."

As Mom pointed toward the windmills, Grace threw her arms around me. "Why, it is my friend Felix from Toledo," she exclaimed. "How nice a surprise to see you again! And wearing such beautiful earrings. You look like a *gitana*, a gypsy."

"Do you know Felix?" Mom asked Grace, obviously surprised.

"Of course," I said, my mind racing with images of myself as a gypsy, dancing barefoot around a campfire, my long skirt swirling gracefully, or wearing a bright scarf and reading people's fortunes in crystal balls.

"She's the person who brought Amy and me back to the Alcázar yesterday when we were lost," I said aloud, "the one I was trying to tell you about. Don't you remember?"

"Oh, yes," Mom said and began thanking Grace.

"De nada, de nada," Grace said. "It was nothing. No trouble."

While Mom and Grace talked, I leaned against the parapet and stared at the distant windmills. As happy as I was to see Grace, I was puzzled. I'd told her we were going to Segovia. Why hadn't she said she was coming here, too? I wanted to ask her, but Mom was monopolizing the conversation.

"Well, Felix," Mom said, finally remembering me. "I think we've seen enough of the castle. I'd like to go into Segovia and see the old Roman aqueduct."

She smiled at Grace. "Thanks again for bringing Felix and Amy back safely. We were so worried about them."

"It was my pleasure," Grace said. "This child, your daughter, was a delight for me to meet. You are lucky to have her."

Mom hugged me. "Felix is very entertaining," she said. "I hope she didn't talk your ear off."

"Everything she said was of interest," Grace assured Mom, and I held my breath, hoping she wouldn't repeat any of our conversation. "I found her most congenial, polite, and friendly," she added, sparing Mom the details.

Mom smiled and nodded, but I thought she looked a little surprised to hear Grace praising me. Usually Amy was the one singled out for compliments, not me.

"Let's go, kids," Don said, summoning Amy and Phillip who were keeping their distance from Grace.

"Remember the view from the river," Grace told Mom. "You must not miss it. You look up and there is the castle high above the trees on its rock, a place of magic, not of the real world but of the air."

Then Grace was gone, vanishing into the crowd as quickly as if she herself were of the air — a woman of magic unlike the tourists milling around, posing for pictures, getting in between Grace and me.

"Where did she go?" I stared at Mom. "I wanted to invite her to have dinner with us."

Mom looked around, as puzzled as I was, but there was no sign of her, not even on the crowded stairs.

.

Unhappy because I'd lost Grace again, I followed Mom out of the castle. Ahead of us, Amy was walking with Don, clinging to his hand while Phillip ran toward a souvenir stand. Amy's long hair swirled out as a gust of warm wind caught it, and Mom gave me a little squeeze.

"Are you and Amy getting along any better?" she asked.

I shook my head. "She hates me."

"Oh, Felix," Mom sighed. "I know it's not all your fault, but I don't think either of you has made any effort to like the other. Couldn't you try a little harder?"

"She's stuck up," I said, "and conceited."

Mom shook her head. "She's just as lonely for her

mother as you are for your father. Can't you see that? She thinks I'm coming between her and Don, and you think Don's coming between you and me. But all Don and I want is to be parents to all three of you."

Mom looked into my eyes, but I lowered my head, refusing to meet her gaze.

"We want to be a family," Mom tried again.

I nodded, but I thought it would take a lot to make us into a family. It certainly wasn't going to happen overnight.

7

After we got into the car, Don drove down a winding road to the river. When we reached the place Grace had described, he parked in a deserted dirt lot, and we all piled out of the car to take pictures. Just as Grace had promised, the castle towered high above us like the figurehead of a ship carved from rock. In the afternoon sunlight, the turrets shone as if they were made of gold, and the whole building looked as if it might vanish in a puff of smoke.

As I pointed my camera upward, I heard Amy mutter, "Oh, no, not her again."

Spinning around, my picture forgotten, I saw a dusty old Citroen pull into the lot and park next to our little red car. Her long hair flying, Grace hurried toward us.

"Oh, Felix," Mom said. "Look who's here."

Grace smiled at us. "Yes, it is me again, a bad nickel you cannot lose," she said. "I have thought more of the windmills and how I would like to show them to you."

"Real windmills," Mom added. "Like the ones in *Don Quixote*."

Grace nodded enthusiastically. "And old castle ruins too. There is so much to see for those who venture from the main roads."

Mom looked at Don before answering Grace. "It's getting late," she said reluctantly, "and we still have to line up a hotel for tonight. I don't think we can see any more sights today."

"Will you be here tomorrow?" Don asked.

Grace sighed and shook her head. "It is impossible. I can take you this one time only."

Mom hesitated, waiting for Don's opinion, and Grace added, "It is too bad, for these are very special. Not the windmills everyone knows. There will be no tourists getting in the way, ruining things, just us."

"Can we go, Mom?" I tugged at her hand, trying to get her attention. "Please?"

While I begged, Grace tapped a long, scarlet fingernail against her front teeth and frowned as if she were thinking hard. Then she smiled. "I could take the children," she offered, "while you go to the hotel and make your reservation. Then, tomorrow, they could show you the way."

"Oh, no," Mom said, "you must have other things to do. We couldn't let you inconvenience yourself like that."

Grace tossed her hair and shrugged. "No trouble, none at all. I would love to show the children the true *España*."

Suddenly Grace's arm hooked around me and drew me to her side. Considering how thin she was, she was surprisingly strong.

"You would like to see my Spain, Felix?" Grace's face

was close to mine, and I could see the pores in her skin, her freckles, and the sun lines around her eyes.

I nodded my head so hard I could feel my big gold earrings swing. More than anything in the world I wanted to see Grace's Spain, to ride in her little car, to talk to her some more. This time, I wouldn't tell her any lies. Just the truth.

"Well, then, you shall." Grace smiled at me as if everything were settled. "I can bring them back to this place at seven-thirty," she said to Mom and Don. "That will give you plenty of time to make the reservation, and perhaps have a glass of wine in a romantic place, just the two of you. Segovia is a city for lovers, you know. A place of beautiful sunsets and ancient things. It would be a shame to miss this chance."

While Mom and Don hesitated, Phillip said, "Let Felix go see the dumb old windmills, if she wants to. I'd rather find a McDonald's."

Grace laughed and drew him close with her other arm. "I know where one is, *señor*. On the way back, we will stop there and you can eat all the burgers you want."

"All right!" For the first time since we'd left Maryland, Phillip looked truly happy.

"Well, I'm not going!" Amy folded her arms tightly across her chest and scowled at Phillip as if he'd just broken a promise. "We can see plenty of windmills tomorrow in Ávila."

But Mom and Don weren't listening to her. This was their honeymoon, and here was Grace offering them a few hours of privacy. Tempted as they were, I had a feeling from the glance they exchanged that they were about to say no. After all, they didn't know Grace very well. How did they know they could trust her?

"Please, Mom," I said. "Grace will take good care of us. Didn't she bring us back safe and sound yesterday?"

Mom looked at Don. Slowly her frown melted into a smile. As Don hugged her, she said to Grace, "If you're sure it's no trouble, I think the children would really enjoy themselves."

"These three trouble?" Grace tightened her grip on Phillip and me and smiled at Amy. "They are splendid children, magnificent children. I will take care of them as if they were my own."

"You'll behave, won't you, Felix?" Mom asked. "You'll stay with Grace and do what she says?"

"And, you," Don said to Phillip. "No climbing on walls, no running off, no silly stunts."

As Phillip and I promised to be good, I saw Amy slip her hand into Don's. "I don't feel good," she said. "Can't I go with you to the hotel? I won't bother you, I promise. I'll go to my room and lie down. You won't even know I'm there."

Don sighed. "Oh, Amy," he said. "Don't spoil things. Go with Felix and Phillip. I'm counting on you to keep an eye on your brother."

With great reluctance, Amy let go of Don's hand and trudged toward Grace's car, pausing every few steps to look back at Don. "I don't want to go," she pleaded.

Ignoring her unhappiness, Don smiled and waved at Amy. "We'll see you soon, sweetie," he called, hugging Mom with his other arm. "Have fun."

Phillip climbed into the back seat and I chose the front, the place of honor beside my friend, the citizen of the world.

As Amy hesitated, Grace revved the Citroen's engine. "Come, Amy," she said, "we must get there before the sun sets or we will have driven in vain to see the windmills."

"Who cares?" Amy said as she got in next to her brother and slammed the door.

Although I was happy to be with Grace, I looked out the window at Mom before we left. She smiled and waved and I waved back. But, even before we were out of sight, she turned to kiss Don.

"At least we won't have to watch that stuff for a while," Phillip said as Grace headed the car away from Segovia.

Amy said nothing, but I silently agreed with Phillip — surely for the first time.

8

As Grace's little car bounced along the road, leaving Mom farther and farther behind, I told myself I had a new friend now, someone who thought I was "magnificent and splendid." She was taking me to see her Spain, the true Spain. Why should I care what Mom and Don were doing? At last I was with someone who appreciated me.

Focusing my attention on Grace, I noticed she was wearing a different tee-shirt today, even more faded than the one she'd worn yesterday, but her jeans were the same. I recognized the hole in the right knee. She had a new flower in her hair, a pale pink one with a red center. Staring intently through the mud-spattered windshield, she looked as beautiful and mysterious as ever.

"I was glad to see you again," I told her. "Why didn't you tell me you were coming to Segovia too?"

Grace shrugged. "It was sudden my coming, a thing of impulse. Yesterday I myself did not know."

I nodded, thinking that made sense. A free spirit had no schedule, no place to go every day like clockwork. To Grace, life must be one long vacation.

"Did you think you'd see me today?" I asked.

Grace glanced at me. "Fate is strange," she said. "I told myself perhaps you would be at the castle, perhaps not. I could not be sure."

"But you were happy I was there, right?"

"Of course," Grace agreed, but she seemed tense, worried. Without saying more, she gripped the steering wheel and leaned forward, watching the traffic and the road. Her mood had changed after we'd gotten into the car. She wasn't laughing or smiling or even talking.

As the silence lengthened, I felt my stomach tighten. Had I offended Grace? Or, worse yet, had Mom said something to make her think we weren't Dallas-style millionaires after all? Maybe she knew what a liar I was and hated me for it.

"Guess what?" I asked, trying to win Grace's approval again. "When I grow up, I'm going to be a citizen of the world just like you. I'll go wherever I want and see everything. Maybe we'll run into each other at the pyramids or someplace. That is, if fate allows it."

Grace looked at me and frowned. "I think you will not be like me, Felix."

I waited for her to say more, but, without another word, she turned off the highway on to a narrow dirt road leading toward the hills. "The windmills, they are this way," she said as we bounced over the ruts.

"What do you mean I won't be like you?" I said, trying to keep the hurt out of my voice. Did Grace think I was just an ordinary kid, an Amy whose one ambition was to be a cheerleader? "I'm going to see the whole world," I told her. "Maybe I'll ride a bike or a motorcycle or maybe I'll hitchhike. I might even get a car just like this one."

When she heard this, Amy sighed so loudly that Grace glanced at her in the rearview mirror. Then she shook her head again. "My life is not what you imagine," she said to me. "It is not all romance and mystery and adventure, Felix."

"I bet it's a lot more exciting than staying in the same old place like my mother. This is the first time she's ever gone anywhere except Ocean City, Maryland. I don't want to end up like her."

Grace frowned at me. "Your mother is very fortunate. She has a good man to love her, a big house, pretty clothes, money for this trip. She has never known poverty or war. Her life is safe, sheltered, protected. And so is yours. Many children are not so lucky, Felix."

As she spoke, I noticed how tightly Grace was clutching the steering wheel. Her voice rose too, and she sounded angry. Worried that I was making things worse, not better, I slumped in my seat and wished I could think of a joke to tell, a funny story, something to make Grace laugh. But nothing came to mind, and I began to think nobody in the car liked me. Not Grace, not Phillip, certainly not Amy. They all hated me.

Suddenly Grace reached over and patted my knee. "I did not mean to upset you, Felix," she said. "I only intended to say your mother is lucky to have what she has. Especially you. I do not understand why you complain, that is all."

As I turned to her, Phillip leaned over the seat and

shouted in Grace's ear. "I'm starving. Couldn't you take us to McDonald's before we see the windmills?"

"How much farther is it anyway?" Amy asked. "You promised we'd be back at seven-thirty."

By then we'd been driving for at least half an hour, taking one turn after another until I had no idea which direction we were going.

"Not far now, not far," Grace said as she negotiated a sharp curve. A herd of cattle watched us jolt past, their faces bored, their jaws working hard like people chewing gum.

"Are you sure we're not lost?" Phillip asked.

Uneasily I looked out the window. The countryside was dry and desolate. Not a town or a building in sight. In fact, the cattle were the only living things we'd seen since we turned off the highway.

"It's going to be dark soon," Amy said. "How will you see the road at night?"

Suddenly Grace leaned forward and pointed. "There, there they are," she said, "the windmills, you see? Straight ahead. Like *Don Quixote*."

Sure enough, three windmills stood above us high on a hilltop, their shapes dark against the rosy sky. From here, with a little imagination, they could be mistaken for monsters. I could almost see the man from La Mancha galloping up to them, brandishing his spear.

"Let us look at them quickly," Grace said as she parked at the bottom of the hill. "Then we shall return to Segovia."

"It is the true *España!*" I cried as I leapt out of the car, eager to impress Grace.

"Watch out." Phillip pushed past me rudely and raced ahead. By the time I caught up with him, he was taking a picture of the windmills.

"Do you like them, Felix?" Grace stood beside me, her hands in the back pockets of her jeans. The sunset blazed in her hair and tinted her shirt as pink as the flower over her ear.

"Oh, yes," I said, wishing she would look at me instead of staring at the sky. "They're so *Spanish.*"

Grace nodded and glanced behind her, down the hill at the little Citroen. She opened her mouth to speak but Phillip ran toward us, interrupting her.

"All my film's gone." He waved his camera in Grace's face. "Can we find that McDonald's now?"

"Yes." Amy looked at her watch. "It's six-thirty."

"You know what's wrong with you two?" I said to Amy and Phillip. "You have no soul."

Amy gave me what she thought was a withering look. "Can't you ever stop showing off, Felix?"

"You're such typical tourists," I said scornfully.

"Oh, look who's talking," Amy said. "The great world traveler, Felicia Flanagan."

Ignoring Amy, I glanced at Grace, but she was already walking down the hill, her back to me. From the way she acted, you'd think I was no more interesting than Amy and Phillip. Why had she bothered to bring me here if she wasn't even going to talk to me?

I watched Amy and Phillip run ahead of Grace toward the Citroen. Then, turning my back on all three of them, I stared at the sunset till my eyes stung with tears. The whole sky was a brilliant pink. Purple clouds massed on the horizon, just above the mountains, and everything glowed with reflected light. All that was missing were cherubs and angels and saints smiling down from heaven.

"Hurry, Felix," Grace called. "You must not delay us."

Reluctant to leave, I walked slowly down the hill, kicking at stones and taking my time. Suddenly I heard the sound of an engine. Looking up, I saw an old Volkswagen bus crest a hill and bounce down the road toward us. It skidded to a stop beside the Citroen, and a man leapt out. He was wearing a stocking over his head and there was a gun in his hand.

At the sight of him, Amy screamed and Phillip tried to run. To my astonishment, Grace grabbed Phillip and then turned to me.

"Come, Felix, *¡este momento!*" she yelled.

When I hesitated, too startled to move, the man with the gun ran up the hill toward me. For a second, I lost all sense of reality. Surely this couldn't be happening. Not to me.

As the man came closer, my heart started racing, my legs shook, my mouth went dry. Without another thought, I spun around and ran up the hill toward the windmills.

Behind me the man shouted. "*¡Deténganse!*"

I didn't know what that meant, so I kept going as fast as my trembling legs would take me.

"No, Felix," Grace called. "Do not cause trouble!"

Pausing for a second, I looked back. Grace's hair caught the last light of the sun and shone as red as fire. From where I stood, I could see the fierceness in her face. There was no lie I could invent to explain her behavior. Grace was helping the man in the stocking mask. She had betrayed me.

I wanted to scream every bad word I knew at her, I wanted to tell her how horrible she was. But I didn't dare. I'd reached the top of the hill and I was skidding down the other side with the man right behind me.

Then I stumbled and fell. Before I could get up, the man had me by the arm. Yanking me to my feet, he said something in Spanish and pushed me up the hill ahead of him.

As he shoved me toward the Volkswagen, I heard a sound overhead. Far above us a jet streaked by, leaving a vapor trail like a chalk mark scratched on the brilliant sky. In it were people, I thought, looking down at the mountains, never dreaming that a kidnapping was taking place beneath their very eyes.

9

When I was thrust, kicking and screaming, through the side door of the Volkswagen, I saw Grace sitting in the driver's seat, her face as white as Phillip's. Beside her was another man. He too was wearing a stocking over his head, but his black leather jacket looked very familiar.

"That was not wise to run, Felix," Grace said softly. "Please cooperate now. You must not anger anyone. Do you understand?"

Ignoring her plea, I leaned over the seat and glared at her. "How could you do this?" I cried. "I thought you were my friend!"

"Sit down," the man in the black jacket said, "beside the other two. And don't be such a bloody little nuisance." He sounded like a British actor on *Masterpiece Theater*, but the gun he held was very real.

Ignoring him, I yanked one gold hoop out of my ear and then the other. Fighting back tears, I hurled them at Grace. "You're right," I said, "I don't want to be anything like you, not now, not ever!"

Without looking at Amy or Phillip, I threw myself down

next to them and stared at the back of Grace's head. At that moment, I hated her with all my heart.

Hearing a car engine start, I glanced out the window and saw the other man at the wheel of the Citroen. He was still wearing the stocking over his head. From where I sat, I could see a machine gun on the seat beside him.

Then Grace turned the key in the Volkswagen's ignition. The bus jolted and jumped as she struggled to get it into gear. The Englishman said, "Can't you do any better than that?"

She glared at him. "It is an old wreck," she said, "and difficult to start. You know that, Charles."

In a few seconds, the bus sputtered and moved forward, more or less smoothly.

Cautiously I stole a glance at Amy. Her face was ashy white and shiny with tears. "This is all your fault," she said. "I told you she was weird, but you wouldn't listen. I hope you're proud of yourself!"

As Amy began sobbing, I leaned toward Grace. "You better take us back to Segovia," I told her. "My father's an important person and he'll send the Marines after you!"

Charles turned around and squinted at me through his stocking mask. "The Marines can't help you now," he said. "So, if you want to see your parents again, I suggest you behave yourself."

"Yes," Grace said. "You must please be quiet and cooperate. This is not a game."

Beside me, Phillip snuffled and sniffed, and Amy squeezed my arm. "Can't you see you're just making things worse?" she sobbed.

Turning my head away, I said nothing. The bus bounced on, lurching and swaying, climbing slowly uphill, its gears grinding and slipping. Speechless with disillusion, I stared out the dirty window. We were driving deeper into the mountains, not back toward the road.

Glancing at my watch, I saw it was almost seven o'clock. The sun had dropped behind the mountains, and as the sky darkened, a few stars appeared. Mom and Don were probably still drinking wine in a little cafe, enjoying our absence. I wondered how long it would be before they remembered they were supposed to meet us in the parking lot. If they called the police right away, maybe they would find us before anything really horrible happened.

·

After at least an hour of creeping up a steep winding road in first gear, the Volkswagen stopped. Charles got out and came round to the side. Opening the door, he gestured at us. "Come along," he said.

Shivering, I followed Amy and Phillip into the darkness. The night air was cold, and the mountains were a black mass against the starry sky. There wasn't a sign of a house or a town, not a light, not a sound. All around us were rocks. Had they brought us here to kill us?

"This way now, please," Grace said, touching my shoulder lightly.

I hesitated, and Charles nudged me forward with his gun. "Go," he said, as the lights of the Citroen swept over us.

"Into the cave," Grace added.

Amy whispered when she saw the small, dark opening

in the rocky hillside, but she dropped to her knees obediently and crawled into it. Phillip followed her.

"You," Charles said to me. "After your brother."

"He's not my brother," I said, but I did as I was told.

After creeping on my hands and knees for several yards, I found myself in a large cavern, dimly lit by a fire burning on a hearth. An old woman dressed in black was stirring something in a pot. She glanced at us, but her face was expressionless. In the flickering light, she looked like a witch.

"Sit down over there," Grace said, brandishing a flashlight. "Against the wall."

"You're making a big mistake," Amy sobbed. "We aren't rich. Felix was lying."

"All Americans are rich, compared to the rest of the world," Charles said. "If your parents can't pay, your government will."

Turning away from us, he said something in Spanish to the old woman. She picked up a ladle and began spooning food from the pot into bowls. Despite everything, I could feel my stomach rumbling. Like Phillip, I'd been hungry for hours.

"Yuck," Phillip said as he poked the stew in his bowl. "What's in this?"

"Goat meat," Grace said, licking her fingers. "Very good."

Phillip tasted a small mouthful and spat it out. "It's awful," he said. "I'm not eating it!"

Amy leaned toward him and grabbed his shoulder. "Do what they say," she whispered. "Don't make them mad."

Putting a forkful of stew in her mouth, she chewed slowly. Then, with tears running down her cheeks, she forced herself to swallow it.

"We don't have to do anything they tell us," I told Phillip. "If you don't like it, don't eat it."

Pushing my bowl away, I glared at Grace. "I'd rather starve than eat this," I said.

"Fine." Charles took my stew, and I sat there listening to my insides growl while Amy and Phillip choked down their dinners.

I wanted to cry, but I wasn't going to give Grace or Amy the satisfaction of seeing my tears. To keep myself from falling apart, I stared at the floor and concentrated on hating Grace.

The next time I looked up, Charles had taken off his stocking mask and was eating my share of the stew. Just as I'd thought, he was the man in the black leather jacket I'd seen last night in the Plaza de Zocodover, the one Amy thought was admiring her.

I glanced at her to see if she'd recognized him yet, but she was still crying into her stew.

When I looked back at our kidnappers, I realized I had other things to worry about. The man who'd caught me had taken off his mask, and I recognized him too. He was the one I'd locked eyes with in Toledo. His cobra stare was as cold as ever, and I shivered, knowing that this time I couldn't just walk away from him. This time I was trapped.

10

After everyone except me had eaten, the old woman collected the plates. In the silence, I could hear the tin utensils clink as she washed them in a bucket of water.

After a while, Charles turned to Grace. "Get their passports," he said.

"Don't give them to her," I told Phillip and Amy, but Amy was already pulling her little canvas purse out of her shirt. Like Phillip's and mine, it hung on a cord around her neck and held her passport and money. Don had bought one for each of us at Wilderness Supplies before we left for Spain, and I could still hear him saying to me, "Whatever you do, keep this hidden under your clothes so a pickpocket can't get it." Until now, I'd thought losing your passport was the worst thing that could happen to you in Spain.

Nervously, Phillip looked from Amy to me and back at Amy. When she saw him hesitating, Amy said, "Give her your passport."

"No!" I grabbed Phillip's hand to stop him, but he ducked away from me and gave Grace what she wanted.

Then it was my turn. "Cooperate, Felix," Grace said. In the flickering light from the fire, her high cheekbones gave her face a cruel quality I'd totally missed in the sunny streets of Toledo.

"I'm not giving you anything," I said to Grace.

"The passport, please," she said.

"No!" I was shouting now.

"I'll take care of this." Charles pushed Grace aside and scowled down at me. "Hand it over," he said.

I ducked but not quickly enough. Charles grabbed the cord around my neck and jerked upward, pulling the purse out of my tee-shirt and over my nose so hard tears stung my eyes.

"I told you, Felix," Grace said. "Do what you are told and you will not be harmed."

"I hate you, I hate you, I hate you!" I screamed and threw myself at her, kicking, scratching, slapping at whatever part of her I could reach.

Then someone grabbed me and pulled me away from Grace. I could smell garlic on his breath as his fingers dug into my skin. It was the man with the cobra eyes. While I struggled to escape, Grace said, "Don't hurt her, Orlando. Please don't. She is a child, remember."

Orlando pushed me away and I reeled across the cave and fell hard on a pile of old blankets. I hurt all over, but I forced myself to sit up and glare at Orlando. I wasn't going to let him know he scared me.

But Orlando wasn't even looking at me. He was studying our passports, frowning and mumbling as Charles tried to explain something to him in Spanish. Grace glanced at me, saw me staring at her, and turned away.

The old woman was sitting quietly by the fire. From the expression on her face, I was pretty sure she was upset about the way Orlando had treated me.

While Charles and Orlando talked, Grace bent over Amy and Phillip. "You must sleep now," she said, pointing to the blankets I was sitting on. "Over there with Felix."

Obediently, Amy and Phillip crossed the cave and sat down beside me. Amy was still crying, and Phillip was very pale.

"You expect us to sleep on these rocks?" I glared at Grace.

Without answering, she dropped the armload of extra blankets she was carrying and walked back to the fire.

"Thank you," Amy said to Grace. Then she handed half the pile to Phillip. "Lie down," she whispered to him.

"Can't we at least have a pillow?" I yelled at Grace.

"Felix!" Amy begged. "Stop it. Do you want to get us killed or something?"

"Be thankful you have blankets," Charles said. "And full stomachs. Many of the world's children would envy you."

"Thank you," Amy said again, to Charles this time. "Thank you for the nice blankets and the good dinner."

I stared at Amy in disbelief. "Don't grovel like that," I hissed. "It's positively disgusting."

She looked at me, her eyes brimming with tears. "I don't know about you," she whispered, "but I want to stay alive. You just keep making things worse and worse. Please, Felix, can't you be nice for once in your life?"

Across the cave, Orlando said something in a low voice, and Grace blew out the candles, leaving only the firelight to illuminate the darkness.

For a while the three of us were silent. Phillip and Amy huddled close to each other, but I sat alone and watched Grace and her friends. They were talking so loudly in Spanish I was sure they were arguing. If only I'd listened to Phillip's tape on the plane to Spain instead of wasting my time reading fashion magazines, then maybe I'd know what was going on.

Reluctantly I asked Phillip, the language expert, if he understood anything Grace and the others were saying.

The firelight shone on his glasses, hiding his eyes, as he leaned toward me. "I can't understand everything," he admitted, "but I think Orlando's going to drive the Citroen back to the main road and leave it far away. Then they're mailing our passports to the U.S. Embassy, along with a letter demanding three hundred thousand dollars."

"One hundred thousand each?" I sucked in my breath. "Wow, they must think we're worth a lot."

"I wonder where they got that idea." Amy glared at me. Turning back to Phillip, she asked, "What are they talking about now?"

Phillip listened hard. After a while he whispered, "Grace wants Orlando to promise he won't hurt us if they don't get the money." He bit his lip. "I think she's afraid he'll kill us if anything goes wrong."

Amy closed her eyes for a moment as Orlando's voice got louder and louder.

"He just said something about *muerte* — 'death.'" Phillip looked at Amy and me.

"They won't hurt us if we cooperate with them," Amy said. "You heard Grace. Just do what they say, Felix, and stop showing off."

I shook my head. "Don't be so dumb, Amy. It doesn't make any difference how good we are. If things go wrong, they'll kill us."

"So what should we do?" Phillip stared at me as if he thought I'd already worked out a plan to save his life.

"Don't listen to Felix!" Amy warned him. "This whole thing is her fault. She's the one who lied about being rich, she's the one who wanted to see the windmills, she's the one who's making them mad. Do what I tell you, Phillip. Be nice."

Phillip looked at me again, his glasses winking in the firelight. "Even if they get the money, they could still kill us." His voice began rising to its familiar whine and I wanted to shake him and Amy both. "That's what happens in the movies."

"Phillip's right," I told Amy. "What's going to stop them from killing us? We have to get out of here," I said, startling myself with my own daring.

"But how?" Phillip quavered. "How, Felix?"

Visions of escape raced through my head. We could grab Orlando's gun, we could throw ashes in their faces, we could extinguish the fire. Once outside, we'd steal the bus and drive to safety in a hail of bullets. I would be at the wheel, of course, while Phillip and Amy cowered on the floor. As we roared into Segovia, Amy would finally acknowledge my skill and bravery. In gratitude, she would kiss my hand and beg me to forgive her for all the unpleasant things she'd said to me in the past.

"How?" Phillip asked again, louder this time.

As I opened my mouth to tell him, I saw Orlando leap to his feet. "¡*Silencio!*" he shouted across the cave at us.

Ignoring me, Amy grabbed Phillip and pulled him down beside her. "Do what Orlando says," she whispered. "Be quiet and go to sleep."

I lay down too, but instead of falling asleep, I thought about my daring plan. In a way I was glad I hadn't said anything to Phillip. The more I thought about it, the more problems I saw. For one thing, I didn't know how to drive. Maybe I would have to work out something a little less risky.

While I lay there, I saw the old woman gather some things together and leave. Then the others smoked a few cigarettes and shared a bottle of wine. Finally Grace and Charles crawled into sleeping bags by the fire, and Orlando took a post by the entrance to the cave. Even in the dark, I could see on the machine gun cradled in his arms. There certainly wouldn't be any sneaking past him.

Unhappily I forced myself to close my eyes and lie still. But all I could hear was my own voice, babbling on and on, making up one lie after another, giving Grace all sorts of false ideas about us. How could I have been so stupid?

*

Much later, something woke me up. Peering into the cave's darkness, I realized that Orlando and Charles had changed places. Charles sat by the cave's entrance, and Orlando snored by the fire.

But it wasn't Orlando who had disturbed me. It was Grace. Huddled next to Charles, she was arguing with him.

"You promised not to tell Orlando of our plan," Grace was saying. "You know I do not trust him so much as this." She snapped her fingers in Charles's face.

"He's the only one who knows how to manage this sort of affair," Charles said. "You and I are bumbling amateurs."

"Yes, but we would not harm anyone, you and I. We agreed there would be no guns, no danger to the children, and what do I see when the Volkswagen arrives? First there is Orlando, then guns, masks, ugly words. And now he talks of keeping the money instead of giving it to the starving children as we planned."

Grace took Charles's hand. "You must not let him ruin things or harm the ones we hold captive. They are children, too. We cannot help the African babies and hurt these three."

Charles sighed and drew Grace close. "Come, come, my dear," he said. "Your idealism is admirable, but three hundred thousand dollars can't feed all the world's children. Split three ways, however, it can give us a very nice life."

Instead of kissing him, Grace shoved Charles away and leapt to her feet. "Traitor!" she cried. "We did this to save the innocents, not to live like degenerates! I cannot believe what I hear from you!"

When Orlando sat up and began mumbling in Spanish, Charles pulled Grace down beside him. "Shh," he implored her. "Don't upset him."

"I care not about his upset," Grace said, but Charles held her tightly as Orlando approached them.

"Let me go!" Grace cried.

"El amor," Charles said to Orlando. *"¿Para qué sirve?"*

The two men laughed, and Charles released Grace. Then he handed Orlando a bottle of wine.

I didn't understand what Charles had said, but it seemed to have satisfied Orlando. Without saying another word, Grace lay down by the fire, and Charles and Orlando smoked and drank together till I finally fell asleep again.

11

The next thing I knew, someone was shaking me. I opened my eyes and saw Grace bending over me. "Time to wake, Felix," she said. "Señora Perez has made a breakfast for you."

Across the cave, the fire was burning brightly, and the old woman was stirring something in her witch's cauldron. Phillip and Amy huddled at her feet, spooning food into their mouths, and Charles and Orlando sprawled nearby, drinking coffee. I had slept more soundly than I thought.

As Grace straightened up, I sprang to my feet and grabbed her arm. "How could you do this?" I whispered, feeling tears burn my eyes.

She tried to pull away, but I hung on to her as tightly as I could. "I stood up for you," I sobbed. "I told Mom how nice you were."

With her free arm, Grace brushed a strand of hair out of her eyes. "Come, please, Felix," she said. "You must eat with the others."

"Aren't you going to answer me?" I thrust myself in front of her as she pulled away from me. "I thought you liked me, I thought I was your friend."

Grace hesitated and looked across the cave at Orlando and Charles. They were talking to each other, paying no attention to Grace and me. "Felix," she said, "you must not take this as a personal thing. In Toledo, you told me you are rich, lots of money, easy life. So I think it is fair to take some of that money to share with other children who are not so lucky. You understand? It was to help the other children that I brought you here. Not to hurt you."

"I heard you and Charles last night," I said. "He and Orlando don't care about starving children. Or us. They just want the money for themselves."

Grace frowned, but before she could answer, Orlando called to her in Spanish. Turning to him she said, "*Un momento, por favor.*" Then she whispered to me, "Do not make that one angry. His temper is bad. You come now and eat. Later we talk, okay?"

Scowling, I let her lead me to the fire. Then I took the bowl Señora Perez handed to me and poked my spoon into the runny porridge. It was lukewarm and full of lumps. If I hadn't been so hungry, I could never have swallowed it.

"This is the worst stuff I ever ate in my whole entire life," Phillip whispered to Amy. "It tastes like pig food."

"Sh," Amy whispered.

Señora Perez was looking at us. "Is good?" she asked.

Amy nodded and smiled as if she were in school, polishing the apple for a good grade. "Thank you very much. *Gracias,*" she added as she gave her empty bowl to the old woman.

Amy nudged Phillip. "Say thank you," she whispered.

Ignoring his sister's instructions, Phillip stuck out his lower lip and silently shoved his bowl toward Señora Perez.

The old woman peered at me. "You," she said, "good?" Like Phillip, I said nothing. I would have liked to dump the porridge in the fire, but I was too hungry for any heroic acts.

A few minutes later, Orlando and Charles prepared to leave the cave. As Orlando puffed impatiently on a cigarette, Charles spoke to Grace softly. Without looking at him, she nodded several times. Her shoulders slumped, her face was pale, even her hair had lost its shine and looked dull auburn in the cave's gloom.

Throwing his cigarette down, Orlando ground it under his heel and growled something to Charles in Spanish. While I watched, his eyes found mine and he frowned. Pulling a revolver out of his jacket pocket, he thrust it toward Grace. His gestures indicated she was to shoot us if we tried to escape.

When she didn't take the gun, Orlando grabbed her shoulder with his free hand and pulled her toward him. With his face close to hers, he shouted at her. Charles tried to intervene, but Orlando yelled at him, too.

"*Dios!*" Charles turned to Grace and began talking rapidly.

With great reluctance, Grace took the gun and nodded as Orlando continued to shout at her.

Finally satisfied that Grace would keep us in the cave, Orlando left. Charles murmured something before following, but Grace didn't answer. Head down, she stood near the entrance, the gun in her hand.

From outside, we heard an engine start, first the tinny sound of the Citroen, then the rumble of the Volkswagen.

Grace stood still for a few seconds longer, listening to the car and the bus chug down the mountain. Then she looked at us, her gaze moving slowly from me to Amy to Phillip and then back again to me.

"Can we go outside for a while?" I asked, forcing myself to speak politely. "I don't think the air in here is good for us. It's cold and damp."

"Yes," Phillip agreed. "It's making me feel sick."

Grace frowned and shook her head. "You must stay in the cave," she said. "Orlando is strict about that."

"But it's so dark," Phillip argued, "and I have to go to the bathroom."

"There is a place for that." Grace pointed to a corner at the back of the cave. "Over there, a bucket behind the curtain."

As Phillip disappeared behind the curtain, Grace looked at Amy and me. "Today Orlando and Charles mail the letter with our demands," she told us. "Perhaps the money will come quickly and you will not have long to stay here."

"Suppose you don't get the ransom?" I asked. "What will happen to us?"

"No harm will come to you," Grace said, but she didn't look at me as she spoke. She sat down cross-legged and laid the gun carefully beside her.

"You'll just let us go, money or no money?" I stared at Grace, wanting to believe her.

Bending her head, she gave her attention to the raveling edge of the hole in her jeans. As she picked at the threads with her long fingernails, she frowned. "We will get the money. Children are important in your country. There will be great demands for your safety."

After Phillip returned from the "bathroom," Grace smiled at the three of us. "You are good children," she said softly. "Please behave, especially when Orlando is here. I swear to you that I will let nothing happen to you."

Picking up the revolver, she got to her feet and we watched her walk away. As she helped Señora Perez with the fire, I sighed. What was I to believe?

Beside me Phillip snuffled and coughed. His eyes were rimmed in red, and his hair stood up in wisps like straw.

Moving closer to Amy, I whispered, "Is Phillip sick?"

She shook her head. "It's his allergies," she said. "Probably the dust and mold in here are making them worse."

"Suppose we tell them he has asthma," I said, "and the cave is bad for him."

"Why?" Amy looked at me suspiciously.

"He could pretend he's having an attack and scare them into letting us go."

"Absolutely not," Amy said. "If you want to get killed, *you* have the asthma attack. Just leave my brother out of it."

Phillip's head swiveled toward us. "Leave me out of what?"

Ignoring Amy, I leaned toward Phillip. "If I tell them you have asthma, can you fake it?" I asked him.

"You mean cough and choke and act like I can't breathe?"

I nodded.

"I guess so," Phillip said. "A boy in my class has asthma, and I know what happens when he gets sick."

"Don't do it," Amy said, but neither Phillip nor I paid any attention to her.

"Should I try it now?" Phillip coughed a couple of times.

"Not now and not ever," Amy said. "I mean it, Phillip."

"No," I said. "Not yet. Let's see what Orlando and Charles say when they come back. Maybe they'll have good news. Or maybe the police will follow them, even."

While Amy tried to convince Phillip not to risk his life, I lay on my blanket and stared at the rocky ceiling, trying to work out a foolproof plan. The trouble was, I had never been any good at thinking ahead. In fact, that was why we were here. It hadn't occurred to me that Amy could possibly be right about Grace. In my eagerness to be with Grace, I hadn't thought ahead. No, I'd trusted her and never once suspected she might not be the person I thought she was.

Now, trying to devise a timetable for our escape, I could imagine the moment when Phillip faked his asthma attack, but after that all I could see was a blur of images. Us running, them chasing us. Shots being fired, bullets ricocheting, shouts and curses, screams. Either we'd be killed or we wouldn't be.

Since I couldn't imagine us dead, I was sure we'd get out of the cave safely. Then, somehow, everything would take care of itself, and we'd be back in Segovia with Mom and Don.

After a while, Amy started crying again. Lying beside her, listening to her sob, I wished I hadn't gotten us into this situation, but I couldn't bring myself to tell her I was sorry. Not while she was being so mean and blaming everything on me. If I apologized, I knew what she'd do. She'd gloat, I was sure she would, and then she'd make me promise to be good. "Be nice, Felix," she'd say. "Do whatever they tell you. Eat goat meat and thank them for it. Don't make them mad."

"Well, I won't be nice," I thought. "Not to any of them."

Across the cave, Grace was sipping a cup of coffee by the fire. "And I'll make you sorry," I silently promised her. "By the time we get out of here, you'll wish you'd never seen us."

Then Grace's eyes met mine. We stared at each other for a moment, and I felt my heart soften. Maybe she was as sorry as I was for the way things were turning out. Maybe she was even sorry enough to help us. Crossing my fingers for luck, I pulled my blanket up around my ears and closed my eyes.

12

I must have dozed off because the next time I looked at Grace she was sitting near the cave's entrance. In the gray light seeping in from outside, her face looked older, not as beautiful as before.

Glancing at Amy and Phillip, I saw they were both sleeping. Getting up quietly, I tiptoed to Grace's side. She jumped when I touched her shoulder.

"Go back and lie down with the others," she said sharply.

"I have to tell you something important." I was close enough to smell the stale cigarette smoke that clung to her hair and clothing. "Phillip has asthma. If he gets an attack, he might die."

Grace stared at me, her pale eyes level with mine. "What do you mean?"

"I mean this cave is bad for him." I paused dramatically and pointed at Phillip who was sitting up now. "Can't you see how sick he looks?" I asked her.

Actually he was no paler or skinnier than usual, but how was Grace to know that?

Grace tapped her fingernail against her front teeth. She looked worried, but before I could tell her anything else, we heard the Volkswagen laboring uphill toward us.

"Quick, go back with the others." Grace gave me a push to speed me up. "Orlando must not see you here with me."

By the time Orlando and Charles entered the cave, Phillip, Amy, and I were huddled together in our corner.

"Is everything under control?" Charles asked. "Did the little blighters give you any trouble?"

"No, they have been very quiet, very good," Grace said. "Even Felix."

Orlando held out his hand for the gun, and Grace gave it to him a lot quicker than she had taken it. As Orlando strode away, Charles patted Grace's shoulder and started talking to her in Spanish.

I turned to Phillip. "What's he telling her?"

He listened for a while. When Charles paused to open a bottle of wine, Phillip whispered, "I think they left the Citroen somewhere with our stuff in it, and they mailed the ransom letter."

Then Orlando took over the conversation, but no matter how hard Phillip tried, he could catch only an occasional word, not enough to understand what the man was saying.

While Phillip struggled to make sense of Orlando's Spanish, I watched Grace. From the expression on her face, I was sure she was arguing with Orlando, but Charles seemed indifferent to both of them. He sat between them, smoking a long, dark cigarette, his narrow face blank. Occasionally he glanced at us the way a person might look at a pigeon or a cow. Not with any real interest, just idle curiosity.

Señora Perez wasn't part of the discussion. She sat near the fire cutting up meat and vegetables. From the way she shook her head and muttered to herself, I felt that she, like Grace, didn't approve of what Orlando was saying.

By the time a pot was simmering over the fire, Charles and Orlando were drinking wine together and laughing as if they were in a cafe. Grace sat apart, her back to them, and smoked one long, dark cigarette after another. Señora Perez continued to mutter and shake her head. Every now and then she looked at us and sighed.

As the goat stew filled the cave with its pungent aroma, Phillip leaned against Amy. "I'm tired of being kidnapped," he said. "I want to go home."

Then he started to cry. Watching tears roll down his cheeks, I felt a big lump form in my own throat. Putting my head on my knees, I began crying too. I couldn't help it. I wanted my mother. I'd had enough, more than enough, of Grace's true *España*.

"Stop it!" Charles said. He was standing over us, frowning. "Stop it immediately. If there's one thing I cannot tolerate it's crying children!"

Orlando scowled at us from the other side of the fire, and Señora Perez muttered glumly, one hand pressed against her forehead, the other stirring the stew. Pushing Charles aside, Grace knelt beside Phillip.

"Now, now," she said, "you must not cry. You will make yourself sick."

Turning to me, she added, "You must set him an example, Felix. Be strong and hard, like the children in my country who fight their enemies and do not cry."

But I had no desire to be like the strong, hard children in Grace's country, whoever they were. Not now, not today. All I wanted was to go home and sit on my mother's lap and be comforted. Pushing Grace's hand away from my shoulder, I kept right on crying.

*

An hour or so later, Señora Perez summoned us to the fire to eat. This time, we took our bowls of stew without complaining. I was so hungry, I would have eaten anything, even brussels sprouts and lima beans. Besides, I told myself, it was better to escape with a full stomach than an empty one.

After dinner, Phillip, Amy, and I retreated to our blankets. In the dim light, I saw Orlando take his post by the cave's entrance. Charles sat silently beside him, smoking one cigarette after another and filling the air with a foul-smelling blue haze. Never in my life had I seen anyone smoke as much as he did. If our health book was right, his lungs must have been coated black with tar. As usual, he also had a bottle of wine to share with Orlando.

Near the fire's smoldering coals, Grace sat alone, her face hidden by her hair. There was no sign of Señora Perez. Perhaps she'd hopped on a broom and flown away.

Finally, too tired to watch my enemies any longer, I

lay down beside Phillip and Amy. They were already asleep, and I envied them. Little fingers of cold air poked under my blankets, and sharp stones jabbed me. Amy moaned and cried in her sleep, and Phillip snored. Worst of all were the rustling sounds in the darkness. Suppose a bear had found its way into the cave? Would it attack me while I slept?

Hour after hour passed. No bear emerged from the shadows. Amy stopped moaning. Except for an occasional snuffle, Phillip slept quietly too. Finally I began to relax, but just when I was on the edge of a dream about home, I felt something bump against me. Terrified, I jerked wide awake and saw Grace's face inches from mine.

"Sh," she whispered as I sat up, too startled to speak. "It is my turn to be the guard, and Orlando wakes easily."

"What do you want?" I stared at her, but she was watching Orlando as if she thought he might throw his blankets aside and mow us down with his machine gun.

When he began snoring, Grace turned back to me. "I am sorry, Felix," she whispered. "You hate me, I know, and believe I have betrayed you. But I did not mean all this to happen."

I frowned at Grace, trying to see her face clearly but the darkness made it impossible. Her features were blurry, her eyes shadowy.

"I thought no harm would come to you," she went on, speaking hastily. "We would get money for the hungry children, the sad-eyed ones with nothing but air in their bellies. Then we would let you go. But now because of Orlando all the plans are changed, and I am afraid."

My heart sped up and my mouth felt dry. "What are you afraid of?" I whispered.

"Orlando is a dangerous man, more dangerous than I thought. He is wanted for robbery and murder, he is a fugitive," Grace said. "And Charles is weak. He will do what Orlando tells him and not argue. His love for me is nothing, no more than this." Grace snapped her fingers under my nose and I jumped. "He cares only for the money and himself. He is not the man I thought he was," she said.

"And you?" I stared at her. "What do you care about?"

"Me?" Grace sighed. "I make no matter in this. What I feel, what I think, is of no importance. To them, I am just a woman. Worthless." She spat into the dust and made a gesture at the sleeping men.

While I sat beside her, trying to understand, Grace lit a cigarette. The match flared and lit her hair, her face, the tears on her cheeks. Was she crying for herself? Or for us?

"If you really care about us, help us escape." I rose to my knees and seized her shoulders. "Please, Grace, please. You've got to help us!"

She pulled away from me and bumped against Phillip. Still asleep, he cried, "Mom, Dad, help."

Instantly Orlando was on his feet, yelling something in Spanish as he strode toward us.

"*El niño,*" Grace said, putting her arms around Phillip. As she spoke to Orlando, I caught the word *asma,* and I knew she was trying to tell him about Phillip.

But Orlando didn't care about anyone's health. Angrily

he yanked Grace to her feet and slapped her hard. Then he turned to the three of us, wide awake now and cowering under our blankets. "¡*Silencio!*" he roared.

Wordlessly, we watched him push Grace back to the fire. Then he sat down at the cave's entrance and made a great show of cleaning and reloading his gun.

When I thought it was safe, I whispered to Phillip, "We're really in trouble."

"I know," he murmured. "Should I fake the asthma attack now?"

"No, not tonight, not while Orlando's here," I said. "Maybe he'll go somewhere with Charles tomorrow. When I think it's the right time, I'll tell you to start coughing and choking. If we cause enough confusion, we can run out of the cave and hide."

"What good will that do?" Amy asked. "We'll just get lost in the mountains and starve to death."

"At least we'll have a chance, Amy," Phillip said. "There must be a village or a farm near here where we can get help."

"But Orlando and Charles have guns," Amy said tearfully, "real guns with real bullets, and we don't have anything."

"Grace will help us," I told Amy. "She doesn't want anything bad to happen to us, I know she doesn't."

We looked across the cave. All we could see of Grace was the hump of her body in her sleeping bag. Charles leaned over her, whispering, but he spoke too softly for us to hear what he was saying.

Not far away, Orlando sat by the cave's entrance. Every now and then he coughed or shifted his position. Sometimes he mumbled in Spanish.

"I'm afraid of him," Amy said. "I'm afraid of Charles too. And, no matter what you say, Felix, I don't trust Grace. You made a big mistake about her once. You could be wrong again." Then Amy lay down and pulled her blanket over her head.

"Are you coming with us tomorrow?" I yanked her cover back and stared at her. "I have to know."

But she wouldn't answer. She just looked at me. Then she rolled over, and all I saw was her back.

"Amy," Phillip whispered. "You have to come. They'll kill you if you stay here."

"They'll kill me if I go," she said.

"Then it doesn't make any difference, right?" I leaned over her so I could see her face again. "If you go. If you stay. It's all the same. Except outside we have a chance of getting away from them. In here, we have no chance."

"Please, Amy, please," Phillip begged. "What will Daddy say if I come back without you?"

"What's going on over there?" Charles called. "Go to sleep right now!"

"¡Silencio!" yelled Orlando.

We lay still for a few minutes. Then I whispered to Amy, "As soon as Phillip fakes his attack tomorrow, run outside and hide."

Amy didn't answer, but I hoped Phillip and I had convinced her to go with us. If Grace helped, we could escape,

I was sure of it. I stole another glance at her, but the cave was so dark I couldn't even see her sleeping bag. There was nothing to do but wait for morning and hope Grace wouldn't let us down.

13

While we were eating our morning porridge, Orlando started yelling at us in Spanish. He looked worse than ever. His shaggy hair and beard were uncombed, and his eyes were bloodshot. When he got no response except a terrified moan from Amy, he beckoned to Charles. They talked for a few minutes, and then Charles walked over and squatted down beside us.

"Orlando's going into town now to see about the ransom," he said. "While he's away, you must behave."

Scowling at us, Orlando handed Charles his gun and said something else.

"I am in charge." Charles looked at everyone, including Grace. "Do you understand?"

When none of us said anything, Orlando nodded grimly. Turning to Grace, he spoke to her rapidly and she mumbled something. Not satisfied, he grabbed her shoulders and shook her roughly as he yelled at her. No one needed to understand Spanish to know he was threatening Grace.

Letting her go, Orlando tucked in his shirt, smoothed

back his hair, and left the cave. Outside, we heard the Volkswagen start and then roar off down the road.

.

Without Orlando, the cave seemed almost peaceful. Charles sat by the entrance, drinking coffee and smoking. Señora Perez tended the fire, sighing from time to time and shaking her head, and Grace sat alone, glancing at us occasionally, her forehead creased with worry.

"I think you should have your asthma attack now," I whispered to Phillip, "before Orlando comes back."

"Don't do it," Amy told her brother. "Charles will know you're not really sick, and he'll shoot you."

"Huh." Phillip glared at Amy. "I fake being sick all the time to get out of going to school, and Dad never suspects a thing. Even you believe me. Anyway," he went on before Amy could interrupt, "I'd rather take my chances with Charles than Orlando."

Without looking at his sister, Phillip started coughing, softly at first, then louder. As he began gasping for breath, Grace and Señora Perez looked at Charles.

"The boy," Grace said. "I told you he has asthma."

Carrying the gun, Charles walked toward us. "Where's his medicine?" he asked me.

His face a convincing shade of purple, Phillip fell to the floor, still coughing.

"It's not here," I told Charles. "He must have left it in the Citroen."

"Do something," Grace said to Charles. "Hold his head up so he can breathe."

Grasping Phillip's shoulders, Charles heaved him upright, but he was hampered by the gun in his hand, and his movements were clumsy. While he bent over Phillip, I shoved him backward as hard as I could.

Taken by surprise, Charles dropped both Phillip and the gun. After kicking the weapon as far from him as I could, I ducked into the tunnel, praying Phillip and Amy were right behind me.

Without looking back, I plunged out of the cave into a gray wall of fog and rain. Unable to see where I was going, I ran blindly, stumbling over rocks and stones. For all I could see, the world ended a few inches ahead of me. Suppose I ran right off the side of the mountain and fell thousands of feet to my death? Suddenly a boulder rose up before me, and I ducked behind it. Crouching down, I felt the strength drain away from me. My arms and legs trembled, my heart thudded, it was hard to breathe. What if the others hadn't followed me? And I was all alone?

Somewhere behind me, I heard Phillip yelling, but the fog hid everything, and I had no idea where his voice was coming from. At least he was out of the cave, I thought, and alive.

Just as my heart was slowing down to its normal rate, I heard Charles shout, "Come back here, you little fools!"

Several shots rang out. I wanted to leap up and run, but I kept my head down and forced myself to stay still. If I moved, Charles would hear me. Even if he couldn't see me, he'd shoot at the noise I made.

Then I saw him less than a foot away, a vague shape blurred by the fog, moving slowly toward me. Holding my breath, I watched him walk past me. He was pointing his gun this way and that like an actor in a war movie. Only he wasn't acting. If he saw me, Charles would shoot me with a real bullet.

When I was sure he was gone, I rose slowly to my feet and peered through the fog. Where were Amy and Phillip? Seeing no one, I crept out from behind my rock and moved cautiously from boulder to boulder, freezing every time a stone rolled out from under my shoes. I wanted to call Amy and Phillip, but I was afraid to raise my voice.

As I edged around a tall slab of rock, I came face to face with Grace. Taken by surprise, I stumbled backward, but I wasn't fast enough. Before I knew what was happening she was pulling me toward her, her hand over my mouth.

"Do not scream," she whispered into my ear. "I am trying to help you."

I nodded, and Grace let me go. "Find a place to hide," she told me, "and stay there. If you run, you will fall and hurt yourself. After dark, go down the road to the village. Be careful. I will do all I can to help."

"Where are Amy and Phillip?" I asked. "Are they all right?"

Grace shook her head. "They ran from the cave like you, but I do not know where they have gone. In the fog, who can tell?"

"Will Charles kill us if he catches us?"

Grace hugged me so tightly I thought my ribs would crack. "Do not think such a thing," she said fiercely. "He could not be that wicked!"

"But Orlando?"

Grace hugged me again. "That one is the devil himself. Go now and hide, Felix, go!"

Then Grace was gone, running away from me and calling, "Children! Children!"

Cold and frightened, I inched my way down the mountainside in the opposite direction, looking for a place to hide. Several minutes later, I found Amy. She was huddled behind a boulder, sobbing. For the first time in my whole entire life I was glad to see her.

"Help me find Phillip," she whispered. "I'm scared Charles shot him."

Taking Amy's arm, I pulled her to her feet. For a second or two she clung to me, shaking. Her hands were icy cold and her teeth chattered so loudly I was afraid Charles would hear them.

"Come on," I whispered. "We'll find him."

But it was Charles we found, not Phillip. In fact, we skidded to a stop not two feet away from him.

Spotting us at the same moment we spotted him, Charles lunged toward Amy and me, but we ducked behind a boulder before he got close enough to grab us. Charles shouted and swore, but Amy and I kept going. We were soaked and cold, and the rocks were slippery, but we weren't about to surrender.

"You stop!" Charles shouted from somewhere in the fog. "Or I'll shoot!"

"*¡Estúpido pulpo!*" I shouted back, remembering Phillip's favorite insult.

At the sound of my voice, Phillip loomed up out of the fog and mist ahead of us. "Quick, this way," he whispered. "I found another cave."

Not too far away, I heard Charles panting and coughing, the result of all those long, dark cigarettes he smoked. "Come back here this moment!" he shouted.

"Charles," Grace called from somewhere. "Over here, quick, I have caught the boy!"

"In here." Phillip grabbed my shirt and pulled me down beside him. On our hands and knees, we wedged ourselves into a tiny cave, barely big enough for the three of us.

Charles passed us twice, calling our names and cursing, but he didn't find us. Once he and Grace actually stopped just a few inches from our hiding place.

"I thought you had the boy," Charles said.

"He got away and then the fog, it swallowed him whole," Grace said. "Now I think maybe he has fallen off the rocks."

"That would be too bloody lovely for words," Charles muttered. "I can't think of a better ending for all three of them. Look at my arm — the little savage bit me. He actually broke the skin. See the blood?"

"Come," Grace said. "We must go back and tell Señora Perez they are gone. Soon Orlando will return. Maybe he will have the ransom, and we can leave this place."

"Do you realize how many germs flourish in the human mouth?" Charles asked. "I'd rather be bitten by a dog than a child. Suppose an infection develops? I could die of septicemia in these mountains."

As the sound of their footsteps faded away, Phillip

turned to me. "I wish he'd get rabies," he whispered. "It would serve him right."

"Now what do we do?" Amy asked Phillip.

"We'd better stay here," I said. "We can't go anywhere in this fog."

"Who put you in charge?" Amy glared at me.

"Look, Amy," I said, trying to sound reasonable. "Somebody has to make the decisions, and it might as well be me. At least I don't sit around crying like a baby the way you do."

Giving me a nasty look, Amy folded her arms around her knees and rested her head on them. In a muffled voice, she muttered something about Miss Know It All. Then she clammed up and refused to utter another word. Phillip and I looked at each other, but we didn't have much to say either.

Silently the three of us sank down into our own thoughts and waited for the long, gray day to end. The only sounds were water dripping through the cracks in the rocks over our heads and occasional rumbles from our empty stomachs. Every now and then I glanced at Amy, but she never met my eyes. Finally, tired, cold, and hungry, I fell asleep.

14

Luckily for us, the fog hugged the mountains till long after dark. Then, all of a sudden, it thinned out into rags and tatters, and a cold wind blew it away. Over our heads, the stars blazed in the clear sky and the moon cast sharp black shadows across the rocky landscape. We shivered, and, when we crawled out of our hiding place, our muscles were so cramped we could hardly stand.

"Where's the cave?" Phillip whispered.

"Over there, I think." I pointed to the left.

"How about the road? Do you see it?" Without waiting for an answer, Phillip scrambled clumsily to the top of a tall boulder and scanned the rocky hillside for signs of a road, a trail, a path, anything that might lead us out of the mountains. But he saw nothing. The landscape was so desolate, we could have been on the moon.

"Maybe we should go back to the cave," Amy said. "We'll freeze to death out here. And I'm starving."

"No," I said. "Orlando will shoot us for sure. Grace told me to go down the road to the village. We can get help there."

Amy opened her mouth to argue, but Phillip interrupted her. From his perch on the boulder, he looked down at us. "I see the Volkswagen," he said.

I climbed up beside him, and he pointed to the old bus nearly hidden by an overhanging rock.

"The road must be there," I said.

"But it's so close to the cave," Amy whispered. "What if they hear us?" She glanced behind her as if she thought Orlando or Charles might appear at any moment.

"We have to risk it," I told her. "It's the only way out of here."

With Phillip and Amy behind me, I crept downhill toward the Volkswagen. The closer we got to the cave, the more scared we were. Fearfully, we slunk from shadow to shadow, trying to avoid the patches of moonlight marbling the ground. Every time one of us kicked a stone loose, we held our breath, waiting to see if the sound would give us away.

We were at the cave's entrance before we realized where we were. Screened by bushes, it was so small a person could pass by without even noticing it. From inside, I heard Charles and Orlando arguing loudly. Grace yelled something at them, and there was a sound of breaking glass. Señora Perez shrieked and Grace swore.

Terrified, we forgot to be cautious and ran the rest of the way to the Volkswagen. As we plunged into its shadow, Phillip tried to open the doors, but they were all locked.

"What are you doing?" Amy pulled Phillip away. "Even if you got inside, you can't drive."

"Sh!" I whispered. "Someone's coming."

We ducked out of sight as a stone rolled out from under a shoe, bounced toward the bus, and pinged against a hubcap. Then Señora Perez came into view, clutching one of her little net grocery bags and muttering to herself.

Thinking she'd lead us to a village, we let her get a safe distance ahead and then inched down the trail behind her. After following her for at least two miles, we saw lights. It wasn't the village we had hoped for but a farmhouse, clinging all by itself to the side of the mountain. Silently, we watched Señora Perez open a gate, quiet the dogs who greeted her by barking, and vanish into the house.

Amy sat down on a rock and started crying. Like her, I was cold, hungry, and scared. The only thing that kept me from crying too was my pride. Biting my lip hard, I forced myself to act brave.

"Come on," I whispered. "We have to keep going. Sooner or later we'll come to the village."

Cautiously, we crept past the farmhouse, trying not to alert the dogs, but it was hard to be quiet on the dark road. Our shoes slipped on the gravel, and soon the dogs, all three of them, were barking and hurling themselves at the stone wall separating them from us. The farmhouse door opened, and Señora Perez shouted something in Spanish.

We ran, plummeting down the steep road, skidding on the loose rocks, breathless with fear. Back up the mountainside we scrambled, seeking a hiding place in the boulders. Even after the sound of the dogs faded away behind us, we kept running.

I paused for breath halfway up a steep hill, and Amy clambered past with Phillip at her heels.

"Wait, Amy," he called. "Wait."

She looked back at him from the top of the hill. "Hurry," she yelled.

Hastily Phillip grabbed at a rock to pull himself up, but it came away in his hand. Before I could catch him, Phillip hurtled backward and tumbled down the hill. By the time I reached him, he was lying on the ground and moaning.

"Are you hurt?" I dropped to my knees beside him and peered at his pale face.

"My ankle," he sobbed. "It twisted when I fell. I think it's broken."

Amy skidded down the hillside and crouched beside her brother. "Are you okay, Phillip?"

He shook his head. "Why didn't you wait? You just kept running and running. I thought you were going to leave me here."

"I'm sorry." Now Amy was crying too. "I didn't think you'd fall, I just wanted you to run faster."

While Amy apologized, I looked behind me, down the mountainside we'd just climbed. Far, far away, I saw the lights of Señora Perez's farmhouse. As I watched, they went out, one by one. The night seemed darker without them. And colder.

"Help me get him on his feet, Felix," Amy said.

Between the two of us we hoisted Phillip up. He put

one arm over Amy's shoulder and the other over mine, but the inequality of our heights kept us from making much progress on the rough, uneven ground.

Soon Amy and I were breathing hard, and Phillip was whimpering with pain. Every time we jostled him, he cried out. "Stop," he sobbed at last. "I can't go any farther."

We eased Phillip down on a grassy mound sheltered by a group of boulders. He leaned against a rock and looked at Amy and me.

"You're going to have to leave me here and get help," he said.

"No, Phillip." Amy shook her head hard. "I promised Daddy I'd take care of you."

"You have to." Phillip's face was ashy white, and his voice shook. "I can't walk, and you can't carry me."

"How can we leave you here all by yourself?" I looked around at the mountains, dappled with moonlight and sharp, dark shadows. It made me shiver just to think about being alone in such a desolate place.

"Suppose wild animals come?" Amy asked.

"Or Orlando?" I would have preferred to face a pack of wolves than the Spaniard. At least animals don't carry guns. And sometimes you can scare them off with rocks.

Phillip scowled at us. "I'm not scared of wild animals," he said. "And Orlando won't find me this far away. I'll be perfectly safe."

I bit my lip and considered the situation. If the three of us stayed here, Orlando would find us eventually — alive or dead. We didn't have food or water, and our clothes weren't warm enough for the night air. How long could we expect to survive?

Then I realized something else. Turning to Phillip, I said, "But you're the only one who knows Spanish. How will we get help without you? How can we explain who we are or what's happened?"

"You'll just have to find someone who speaks English," Phillip said.

"Out here, in the middle of nowhere?" I stared at him. "If you were a Spanish person lost in the mountains of West Virginia, would you expect to find somebody who spoke your language?"

"I told you to listen to my tape." Phillip sounded a bit more like his ordinary self. "But no, all you two did on the plane was read dumb books and magazines."

Frowning, he reached into his shirt pocket and pulled out his little Spanish phrase book. "Here," he said. "Maybe this will help."

As I took the book, Amy and I stared at each other. Over our heads, the stars shone and a half moon gazed down at us. Never had I felt so helpless.

"Go on," Phillip said.

"Are you sure you'll be okay?" I asked him.

He nodded. "Just get me some stones before you go," he said, "so I'll have something to throw if a bear or a wolf comes along."

For several minutes, Amy and I gathered stones and silently piled them up around Phillip. When he told us he had enough, I turned away slowly, clutching the book.

While Amy hesitated, Phillip said, "Will you just go? The sooner you leave, the sooner you'll get some help for me."

Without saying anything to each other, Amy and I walked down the hillside, leaving Phillip behind. I looked back once, and he waved. The moonlight shining on his glasses made it impossible to tell if he were crying or not. But even if he were, he had a lot more courage than I'd thought.

15

It was the first time Amy and I had been alone together since the fateful day we'd met Grace in Toledo. Every now and then, as we stumbled down the rough slope, I'd clear my throat, trying to think of something to say, but the words wouldn't come. For some reason, I just couldn't bring myself to apologize.

Finally Amy broke the silence. "I can't believe this is happening," she said. "It's like a nightmare I can't wake up from."

Glancing at her, I was amazed at the expression on her face. We were lost on a rocky hillside in the mountains of Spain, but, instead of trying to find a way out, Amy was frowning at me as if I were responsible for the entire situation.

"Will you quit blaming me?" The wind was cutting right through my tee-shirt and whipping my hair into my eyes. "I'm sorry, okay? I'm sorry!" I was shouting but I didn't care. "You were right. I shouldn't have told Grace all that stuff."

Amy's hair had fallen out of its barrettes long ago, and the wind had snarled it into a tangled mass. Her face was streaked with dirt and tears, and she was missing one sandal, something I hadn't noticed before.

"If I ever see Daddy again, I'm going to tell him this was all your fault," Amy said.

"I don't care what you tell him, you goody-goody little tattletale," I said. "At least Phillip and I got us out of that cave. If we'd stayed there like you wanted to, we'd probably be dead now."

"Thanks to you, we're probably going to die anyhow." Amy looked back up the mountain as if she were searching for Phillip's hiding place. "I might never see my brother again or Daddy or anybody I care about!"

When Amy started sobbing, I grabbed her arms and shook her. "Stop it," I said, "stop it! Crying isn't going to get us out of here!"

She pulled away from me and stumbled backward uphill. "I hate you," Amy screamed, "I loathe and despise you, Felicia Flanagan!"

"Same here!" I screamed back.

"I hope my father divorces your mother and I never see you again!"

"Same here!"

"If Daddy doesn't get a divorce, I'll go live with my mother!"

"And I'll go live with my father!"

Out of breath and shivering in the cold, we glared at each other. Then I turned and ran down the mountain, hoping I was heading toward the road. As far as I was concerned, Amy could stay in the mountains forever. I'd apologized and look how she'd acted. Just as nasty as ever.

While I was thinking up insults to hurl at Amy, a rock spun out from under my shoe. Flapping my arms wildly, I tried to keep my balance, but I fell anyway and slid several feet downhill on my side.

As I crashed into a boulder, Amy called, "I hope you broke your leg! It would serve you right!"

Ignoring her, I sat up and looked at myself. My jeans were ripped and the skin on my thigh was scraped and raw. Even in the moonlight, I could see blood welling up, black against the whiteness of my flesh. Gritting my teeth, I got to my feet. It hurt, but I could walk.

As I hobbled along, I heard Amy behind me. Wheeling around, I said, "If you hate me so much, how come you're following me?"

Amy gave me a fierce look. "Hating you doesn't have anything to do with it!" she yelled. "I'm scared and I'd rather be with you than nobody!"

Well, I was scared too. In fact, I was just about dead from terror, but I didn't want to admit it to Amy. I stood there, slightly below her on the hillside, listening to my heart thumping hard in my chest. Fighting my desire to throw myself down on the rocks and cry like a baby, I tried to think about our situation sensibly. Here we were, lost in Spain with kidnappers hunting us, and what were we doing? Fighting like little kids.

Swallowing my pride, I forced myself to say, "Maybe we should quit arguing, Amy, and try to figure out what to do."

She rubbed her eyes with her fists and stared at me. "Do you know where you're going?"

"No," I confessed.

"I didn't think so," she muttered.

Without looking at each other, we sat down on a rocky outcropping. For a while neither of us spoke. My leg hurt, and I was cold, tired, and hungry — goat stew, porridge, anything would have tasted good at this point. Finally, my stomach growled so loudly Amy looked at me.

"I've got some cheese crackers," she said. "You can have half." Reaching into her pocket, she pulled out a smashed pack and gave me two crackers.

"I was saving them for Phillip and me," she admitted as I bit into one.

I shrugged and glanced at her, but the wind was blowing so hard her hair hid her face.

"I hope he's okay," she said.

"Me too."

"He must be hungry though. And cold."

I nodded, but I didn't look at Amy. What could I say? I was worried about Phillip too. "We'll find somebody to help us," I said after a while.

Swallowing the last of my crackers, I surveyed the landscape spread out below me. Way off to the right, I thought I saw a cluster of lights. Then very faintly I made out the thin winding line of the road curving around the hills far below.

Nudging Amy, I said, "I think that's the road."

Slowly we got to our feet and began climbing down the hillside. Because my leg was stiffening up, I couldn't race ahead of Amy. By the time we reached the road, I was several yards behind her and limping.

.

After we'd walked for about an hour without seeing a single house, we stopped to rest on a low stone wall. A breeze blew through the olive trees behind us and we shivered.

"I wonder what time it is," Amy said.

I squinted at my watch, trying to make out the numbers. "I think it's around midnight."

"I'm so tired," Amy said. "If only we could sleep for a while."

"Maybe if we walk a little farther, we'll come to a barn or something," I said.

I eased myself off the wall, and Amy and I trudged down the road. We passed a field where a herd of sheep slept as still and white as boulders in the moonlight and another field where cows slumbered — or were they bulls? Finally under a tall tree I saw a small stone stable, far enough from the road to make me feel sure Orlando wouldn't find us there.

We climbed over a wall and crept through the damp grass. Ahead I could see more sleeping cattle, but we edged past without disturbing them and slipped into the stable.

Although its door was gone, it had a roof, and in one corner I saw a pile of burlap sacks. Ignoring their old barnyard odor, we made a nest of them and snuggled down, warmer than we had been before.

"I hope Phillip doesn't freeze up there," Amy whispered after a while.

"The rocks will shelter him," I said. "And the bushes."

Amy was silent, but when I was almost asleep, she turned toward me and asked, "Do you really hope our parents divorce each other?"

I frowned into the darkness. Much as I hated to admit it, my mother loved Don. She'd been so happy when he asked her to marry him. Uncomfortably, I remembered her telling me I was going to have a real family now, a father, a brother, and a sister. But all I'd wanted was Mom. And my own true father, the one who'd gone away when I was three and married someone else. The one who didn't want me anymore.

"Well?" Amy asked when I didn't answer her question.

"What about you?" I stared into the darkness, trying to see her face. I wanted her to answer first, not me. "If they stay together, are you going to live with your mother?"

Amy shook her head. "I'd never leave my father," she said. "Not even if my mother wanted me to."

Amy's voice shook a little, and, after a pause, she added, "My father is the one I love, not my mother. After what she did to Daddy, how could I ever trust her?"

"But your father lives with *my* mother, and that includes me because I'm certainly not going to leave." Like Amy, I hesitated before I added, "My father doesn't need me. He has a new wife and a new baby now. What would he want with me? I'm just his old kid."

"So I'm stuck with you, is that what you're saying?" Amy asked me.

"And I'm stuck with you and Phillip."

There was a little silence. I guess, like me, Amy was thinking about the implications of what we'd just confessed. Then her burlap sacks rustled as she propped herself up to see me better.

Staring directly at me, she asked, "Do you hate my father?"

I thought about Don. He was quiet and shy, kind of like Phillip. Not handsome like my real father, not rich, but not really boring. And Mom was happier now that he was around, I couldn't deny that. Maybe by the time we got back home — if we ever did — I'd be used to sharing Mom with him. I sighed and rearranged my burlap sacks.

"No," I said to Amy, "I don't hate your dad. He's okay most of the time, I guess."

I paused and looked at her. "How about you? Do you hate my mother?"

Amy shook her head. "Actually I kind of like *her*," she said. "Even if she can't cook."

"It's just *me* you don't like." I was sitting up now, ready to get mad again if I had to.

"Well, you don't like me," she said. "Or Phillip. So why should I like you?"

It was a good question but one I didn't want to answer at the moment. In the first place, I'd changed my mind about Phillip. He wasn't so bad after all. And, in the second place, I was even beginning to relent a little about Amy, but she obviously disliked me, so why give myself away? To use her own words, I was a showoff, know-it-all idiot.

Snuggling up in my burlap sacks, I said, "We better get some sleep."

I closed my eyes and waited for Amy to say something

else, but all I heard from her was a sigh. As I lay there, trying to ignore the musty reek of the burlap, I realized I was hoping Amy would come up with some excuse for liking me anyway.

For a few minutes, I thought about telling her I was willing to be friends, but by the time I got the words together it was too late. Amy was sound asleep.

16

When I woke up, it was barely light. For a
moment I was so confused I thought I was
still in the cave. Amy was shaking me, her hair tickling
my face.

"Felix," she whispered urgently, "Felix! Somebody's
outside!"

"Huh? What?" I sat up and pushed aside the evil-
smelling burlap sacks.

Amy pointed at the doorway. As it was yesterday, the
air was foggy gray. Hidden in the mist, someone was definitely approaching the stable. I could hear shuffling footsteps and soft breathing.

"It must be Charles and Orlando," Amy told me. "What
should we do?"

"Stay still," I warned her. "Maybe they won't see us."

But the footsteps came closer. From the sound of them
squish-squashing through the damp grass, I was sure it was
a lot more than two people. Had Charles and Orlando
recruited a whole gang of kidnappers to find us?

Amy and I huddled together, expecting to be recaptured
at any moment. Then I heard it — a low mooing sound.

Opening my eyes, I saw a cow staring through the stable door.

At the sight of its big tan head, Amy and I burst into laughter.

"Cows," Amy giggled. "We've been surrounded by cows!"

"Oh, no," I said, "it's a herd of cownappers. They're trying to horn in on the action." I collapsed on the floor, practically hysterical over my own joke. "*Horn in* — get it?"

Despite the pain in my sore leg, I was laughing so hard tears were running down my cheeks. "They've mined the pasture with their secret weapon — cow plops!"

"Mooooo," the cow said loudly.

"Oh, I'm so sorry, Madame Cow," I said, staring up at its brown eyes. "Did I butt into your private business?"

Right in the middle of a loud guffaw from Amy, I had a thought so terrible that it left me weak in the knees and dry in the mouth.

"Amy," I plucked at her sleeve, afraid to take my eyes off the horned head poking into the shed. "Suppose it's not a cow? Suppose it's a bull?"

Her eyes widening, Amy scrambled away from the door and flattened herself against the back wall. "How can you tell which it is?" she asked me.

I was right beside her, as far from the beast as I could get. "If we could see the rest of its body, we'd know," I whispered, "but all that's showing is its head. Cows' horns aren't that long, are they?"

Amy shook her head. She didn't know any more about cattle than I did.

"Moooo," the beast said. From out in the mist, a little chorus of moos answered.

"If it was Charles, we could at least reason with him," I said. "But what do you say to a bull?"

"And *you* have on a red tee-shirt!" Amy glared at me as if I'd planned the whole thing, right down to my clothes.

"When I put this shirt on in Toledo how could I know I was going to meet a bull?" It was one thing for Amy to blame me for blabbing to Grace, but to accuse me of wearing red on purpose was going too far. Especially when I was beginning to think we might become friends after all.

"Anyway, it's just a myth about bulls hating red," I said. "They're color blind like all animals. Don't you know anything?"

"There you go again," Amy said, "acting like a conceited know-it-all!"

"I can't help being smart," I said.

"Mooooo," the mystery animal said loudly. Then it shook its horns in a distinctly bull-like fashion.

"Shut up, Felix!" Amy yelled. "Can't you see you're making it mad?"

"Moooo!" This time the animal not only shook its horns but pawed the ground daintily with one cloven hoof.

"Stand absolutely still," I whispered. "Don't move or say anything. Maybe it'll get bored and go away."

We stood side by side, petrified. I didn't think the bull

could wedge himself through the doorway, but I wasn't positive.

Just as it was beginning to look as if the animal meant to keep us prisoners all day, something distracted him. He gave us one last, long look, mooed or bellowed — whatever bulls do — and slowly withdrew his head. Turning his back on the shed, he suddenly galloped off, and his buddies followed him. From somewhere a dog barked, and there was a big chorus of mooing.

Cautiously Amy and I crept out of the shed and peered into the mist.

"Can you see them?" Amy whispered.

I shook my head. "Let's get back to the road."

We ran across the grass and scrambled over the wall. Then, breathing hard, we hurried along, listening not only for the bulls but for the Volkswagen bus as well. By sleeping, we'd lost valuable time. And, worse yet, we'd be easier to find in the daylight.

Rounding a curve in the road, we saw a big stone barn looming out of the mist. The cattle milled around in the road, dozens of them, while a dog nipped at their heels, guiding them inside. An old man waved a stick, helping the dog's efforts by calling the beasts by name.

"So that's why they left," I said. "It was feeding time."

We hesitated, not sure we wanted to get any closer. Although I was positive the cattle had come from the pasture we'd just left, I had a feeling they weren't bulls after all. In fact, even from here I could see their udders hanging heavy with milk. Had we been held hostage by a cow after all?

Then the man spotted us and yelled something in Spanish. It didn't sound friendly, and, when he started toward us, Amy and I turned and ran back the way we'd come.

Behind us the dog barked and the cattle mooed. From off to the left, a bunch of sheep, invisible in the morning mist, began baaing, and a flock of crows rose from the olive grove ahead of us, adding their voices to the din.

My leg was so sore that every step was agony, but, once more, I scrambled up a hillside and cowered behind a clump of boulders with Amy.

"Is he coming?" Amy asked.

"I don't see him."

She stared at me. "Do you think he'll tell Orlando where we are?"

"It's possible." I swallowed hard. "For all we know, everyone around here is related to everyone else. Anybody we go to might grab us and hand us over to Orlando."

The clouds sagged down lower and wisps of mist blew between us like tiny clouds. Our clothes were damp, and I felt chilled to my bones.

"You don't have any more crackers, do you?" I asked Amy.

She shook her head. "I'm *starving*."

"Me, too," I said. "Right, now, even Señora Perez's porridge would taste good."

"Or how about an Egg McMuffin?"

"Or a dozen pancakes?"

Both our stomachs growled together, and we laughed at the fierce sound they made.

A few more minutes passed with no sign of the old man

or his dog. "Maybe he's in the barn milking the cows," I said.

"Cows?" Amy stared at me. "Those were cows?"

"The ones in the road were," I said.

"You mean we stayed in that stable because of a dumb *cow?*"

"The one in the doorway was a *bull*," I said. "The others were cows."

"Are you sure, Felix?"

I bit my lip and shook my head. "No," I said, "but whatever it was, it was very big and it had long horns and I wasn't about to push it out of the way."

Amy sighed. "Neither was I."

I smiled at her just a little and she smiled back. Then we climbed down the hill to the road. When we reached the barn, the cattle were out of sight and so were the old man and his dog. As we ran past, I heard a lot of mooing from inside, but no one dashed out into the road to stop us.

When the barn was out of sight, we slowed down again. After walking at least a mile, probably more, we came to the top of a hill. The road dropped steeply away into a valley. Wraiths of fog floated below us, but, from where we stood, we could just make out the red tile rooftops of a small village.

"Let's go," I said, and the two of us, both limping, began to run.

Then we heard the sound of an engine behind us, laboring from gear to gear as it crested the hill.

"Quick!" I grabbed Amy's hand and pulled her off the

road into a ravine. Of course, I tripped and slid on the gravel, and scraped my arm.

Lying still, we watched the Volkswagen bus slowly emerge from the fog, its yellow headlights glowing like tiger eyes. Although we couldn't see who was driving, I was sure I saw Phillip peering out the rear window.

"They've caught your brother," I told Amy.

"Oh, no." She stared at me, her eyes huge in her dirty face. "What should we do?"

I shook my head. "Keep trying to get to the police," I said as the bus vanished into a wall of dense fog.

"Did he look like he was all right?" Amy asked as we crept slowly down the road, fearful of coming upon the bus unexpectedly.

I nodded. "I hope they put a splint on his ankle."

"Poor Phillip, I'll never be mean to him again," she sobbed. "All the times I've teased him and picked on him. Oh, why wasn't I nicer to him?"

I didn't say anything, but I gave Amy a little pat on the shoulder. Since I hadn't been particularly nice to Phillip myself, I was feeling pretty guilty too.

By the time we reached the village, it was after two o'clock, and all the shops were closed for afternoon siesta. On the little balconies overhead, lines of laundry gave a bit of color to the grayness, but, with the exception of pigeons, a couple of thin dogs, and an even thinner cat, I saw no one on the street.

Then we heard a car coming. Afraid it was Orlando, we ducked into a narrow alley. Crouching behind a trio of battered garbage cans, we watched an old Citroen, similar to Grace's, pass us and vanish around a corner into the fog. There was no sign of the bus.

The skinny cat rubbed itself against my legs and purred loudly. While I stroked its bony sides, Amy slumped against a wall. By now she'd lost both sandals. Like me, her clothes were torn and filthy, and her hair was a mass of tangles. We looked like two gypsy beggar girls.

"Come on, Amy," I said. "We can't give up now. I've still got Phillip's phrase book. Maybe if we use it, we can make somebody understand what's happened."

Amy frowned. The skin below her eyes had a bruised look, and she was very pale under the dirt on her face. "Just promise me," she said, "not to ask any red-haired citizen of the world for help."

17

For a minute I was tempted to make a smart remark, but, instead, I said, "I wish you'd forget about Grace. I'm just as sorry as you about what I did."

Amy looked at me. "I guess you are," she murmured.

The two of us walked down the street while I thumbed through the words and phrases in Phillip's book. The first translations were meant to help you decipher a menu, which shows where most tourists' priorities are. Flipping a few more pages, I came to an "A to Z Summary of Practical Facts and Information."

After skimming past directions for renting cars, buying cigarettes, mailing letters, and sending telegrams, I found how to say your passport has been stolen. That was helpful.

"Me han robado el pasaporte," I read out loud to Amy. "Does that sound right?"

She shrugged. "How do I know? I took French One last year."

"Well, how about this?" I asked, pausing on another page. *"¿Dónde esta la embajada americana?"*

"What's that mean?"

"Where's the American Embassy?" I looked farther down the page. *"¡Socorro!"* I shouted. *"¡Policía!"*

Startled, Amy jumped.

"That means 'Help, police,' " I told her.

I flipped a few more pages, pausing at one I thought might interest Amy. "If we want to get our hair done or our clothes washed, I know how to say it," I added.

"Great," Amy said, obviously unimpressed.

"Oh, look, here's what we really need!" I stabbed a line of print on page 118. "*¿Dónde esta la comisaría más cercana?*" I smiled at Amy. "That means 'Where's the nearest police station?' "

With great exaggeration, Amy gazed around us at the deserted street. "And who do we ask? The cat?"

"*El gato,*" I told her, "knows everything, but I don't speak his language."

"You're getting on my nerves, Felix," Amy said. "Whether you want to admit it or not, we're in serious trouble and your dumb jokes aren't helping."

Disappointed by Amy's lack of humor, I marked the helpful pages and shoved the little book back into my pocket. We'd walked three whole blocks now and still had seen nobody. Maybe I was wasting my time.

Just then a door opened a few yards up the street and an old lady dressed in black stepped out into the fog. At first I drew back, afraid it was Señora Perez, but, as she drew nearer to Amy and me, I saw she was a stranger.

"*Perdóneme,*" I said as politely and carefully as I could, but at the sight of me, the old woman darted right past, shaking her head and muttering something in Spanish that sounded like, "*No tengo dinero, no tengo dinero.*"

"*Dinero* — doesn't that mean money?" I asked as the

old woman disappeared around a corner. "I bet she thought we were begging."

"Great," Amy said. "We didn't even have a chance to ask her where the nearest police station is."

"Will you stop being so sarcastic all the time?" I frowned at Amy. "If you want to know, *that* really gets on *my* nerves!"

"So now we're even!"

Without saying anything else, we walked side by side down the narrow street, passing closed doors and shuttered windows. Once a little boy rolled past on a skateboard, but he just laughed when I asked him where the nearest police station was. He didn't even look back before he vanished into the fog.

The street ended in a square containing a cafe, a grocery store, and a *farmacia*, all closed. On benches around a fountain sat five old men, two playing checkers, the others watching and laughing. At the sight of us, they looked at each other and muttered in rapid Spanish.

"*Gitanas*," one said as I approached, phrasebook open to the page about the police station.

"*Socorro*," I said, "*soy americana.*"

"*No tengo dinero*," one gentleman interrupted me before I even got to the police part. "*¡Vamos!*"

"*Por favor*," I tried again. "*¿Habla usted inglés?*"

"*¡Vamos!*" Two of the old men got up and started toward Amy and me.

"*¡Policía!*" I cried, as Amy tried to pull me away. "*¿Dónde esta la comisaría más cercana?*"

But the old men were all shouting now, making no

effort to understand me, and they looked very angry. Scared, I ran from the square with Amy.

"They definitely don't like Americans here," I said as we ran down Calle de los Angeles.

"They don't understand anything you're saying," Amy said. "You might as well give up and throw that dumb book in the trash."

Suddenly I stopped and pulled Amy into an alley. "The Volkswagen's coming!"

We ducked behind a pile of boxes. It was the bus all right, and Grace was driving with Phillip beside her. She was scanning both sides of the street, a frown creasing her forehead. I started to jump up and wave but Amy pulled me down.

"What's the matter with you?" she hissed as I struggled to get away from her. "Are you crazy?"

"It's Grace and Phillip," I told her. "They're looking for us!"

"It's a trick," Amy said. "Orlando and Charles are probably hiding in the back."

"I never thought of that." I listened to the engine fade away into the fog. With the Volkswagen prowling the streets searching for us, how were Amy and I ever going to get back to Segovia?

Then we heard another noise. A real bus was lumbering toward us. It was old and dusty and its sides were plastered with advertisements, but the sign on its front said Segovia.

"Come on, Amy!" Limping out of the alley, we ran after the bus as it vanished around a corner.

When we caught up with it, the bus was sitting all by

itself on the edge of the square. The old men were still playing checkers and kibitzing. They had been joined by three teenage boys on bicycles who seemed to have nothing to do but pedal around the fountain.

Trying to avoid attracting their attention, Amy and I edged along the side of the square, staying close to the walls, hoping the fog would hide us.

"Where's the driver?" Amy whispered as I peered through the open door of the bus.

"I don't see him," I said. "Maybe he went in there."

I pointed across the square at the cafe. Its doors were open now. From inside, I could heard voices. The delicious aroma of hot rolls and coffee wafted through the cool air, and my stomach rumbled so loudly I thought the old men would hear it.

"Do you have any money?" Amy asked.

I felt in my pockets and pulled out some coins. A five-peseta piece, a one-peseta piece, and four twenty-peseta pieces. "Eighty-six pesetas," I said. "That probably won't even buy a cup of coffee."

Amy held out an even smaller amount of coins, totaling fifty-five pesetas. "We don't have enough money for tickets," she said. "What will we do?"

We didn't have time to think about it because just then I saw the Volkswagen coming around the corner.

"Quick!" Grabbing Amy's hand, I yanked her into the bus. Dropping to the floor, we crawled to the back and hid behind the last row of seats.

"Did they see us?" Amy whispered.

"I don't think so." Cautiously I raised my head and

peeked out the window. To my horror, I saw Charles and Orlando walking across the square. I dove to the floor beside Amy, praying they would keep on going.

"We'll have to stay here now," I told Amy. "Just hope nobody wants to sit in the back seat."

At first, I was really scared because I expected Charles and Orlando to get on the bus. But, as time went by and they didn't appear, I started feeling bored and restless. It didn't help to be hungry and thirsty.

Every now and then I popped up and looked out the window, but I didn't see the bus driver or Charles and Orlando. Just the unfriendly old men playing checkers and the boys doing wheelies around and around the fountain.

"Suppose this is the end of the line?" Amy whispered. "And the bus is parked here till tomorrow?"

"Do you have to be so optimistic about everything?" I frowned at Amy, but I couldn't help thinking she might be right.

I raised my head for another peek and saw something that made my stomach lurch. I hit the floor and grabbed Amy's arm. She was staring at me wide-eyed, but for a moment I couldn't force myself to tell her what I'd just seen.

"Charles and Orlando," I croaked, "just came out of the cafe with a man who looks like a bus driver."

After a few seconds of heart-thumping silence, I heard Charles and Orlando talking in Spanish. Without Phillip, I had no idea what they were saying, but I got the feeling they were standing by the open bus door.

Then someone else spoke. His voice was warm and

friendly as he stepped into the bus. Clink clink — money dropped into the fare box, and Charles and Orlando sat down in the front of the bus, probably right behind the driver judging from the sound of their voices.

A few more minutes passed, and several other people got on. A couple of women, a few children, a baby, at least one man, and a couple of teenage boys. To Amy's and my unspeakable relief, all the other riders sat near the front.

As the bus began to move, Amy and I looked at each other. "Why do you think Charles and Orlando are riding this bus?" Amy whispered. "Why aren't they in the Volkswagen with Grace and Phillip?"

I thought about that and then, feeling sort of sick, I said, "Maybe Grace stole it. First she found Phillip, and then she started looking for us."

Amy's tears left white tracks on her cheeks. "Then we shouldn't have hidden from them?"

"I guess not," I mumbled.

As the bus bounced and jolted up a steep road we left the fog behind, but the sunlight streaming through the dirty windows didn't cheer me up. Why had I listened to Amy? If she hadn't pulled me back into the alley, we'd probably be safely on our way to Segovia with Grace and Phillip instead of hiding on a bus with Charles and Orlando.

Just as I was about to tell Amy what a dope she was, there was an outburst of yelling and screaming. The bus swayed hard, and I thought we were about to crash until I heard Orlando shouting. Peeking between the seats, I saw him standing in the aisle and pointing his gun at the passengers. Behind him, Charles had shoved the driver aside and taken control of the bus. Ahead of us I caught a glimpse of the Volkswagen.

Heeding Orlando's orders, the passengers were scrambling over each other in an effort to move to the rear of the bus. In the confusion, two old women tried to slide into the rear seat. They were so busy watching Orlando they didn't notice Amy and me on the floor till they tripped over us.

"*Las niñas,*" one cried, and I recognized the old lady who had mistaken Amy and me for gypsies earlier.

"Sh, sh!" I begged, grateful for the noise of the baby who was crying loudly. Pointing my finger at my head like a gun, I said, "Bang, bang — *muerto!*"

The old ladies stared at me, but two young women, one holding the wailing baby, were wedging themselves into the seat. Trembling and weeping, they distracted the old ladies' attention from Amy and me.

Then a little boy spotted us. I'm sure he called us dirty gypsies, but Orlando wasn't looking our way. To my horror, he was aiming his gun at the Volkswagen. As he squeezed the trigger, our bus's windshield shattered in a shower of safety glass. Everyone screamed at the noise of the gun, and Charles swerved as if the explosion had scared him, too. In fact, he almost lost control of the bus as we skidded around a sharp curve.

Through the broken glass and dust, I saw the Volkswagen disappear over a hill.

"Bloody hell," Charles yelled at Orlando. "Don't do that again! Do you want to wreck the bus, you fool?"

Orlando shouted at Charles in Spanish and Charles shouted back, this time in Spanish. Again the bus careened, the brakes squealed, and the two men cursed.

When a teenage boy lunged forward, Orlando whirled around and pointed the gun at him. He yelled a sentence that had "*muerto*" in it, and the boy slid down in his seat, trying to shield his head with his arms.

As Charles began gaining on the Volkswagen, the bus swayed and bounced violently. Everybody, Amy and me included, rose up in the air and slammed back down as we hurtled madly over ruts and bumps and slid around curves. A grocery bag burst open, and soon we were ducking flying squash, tomatoes, loaves of bread, cans of food, bottles of milk, and a flounder or two.

"*¡Socorro!*" one old woman cried, and the baby's mother screamed louder than the baby itself.

But the bus continued to pursue the Volkswagen, and Orlando fired at it a few more times, paying no attention to Charles's pleas.

Then two things happened at once. As we slid around a curve, I shot out from behind the back seat, and Orlando saw me. At the same moment, Charles lost control of the bus.

18

Orlando shouted and started moving toward me, but he slipped on a smashed tomato and crashed to the floor just as the bus veered off the road and skidded down the hillside.

"We're all going to die!" Amy screamed as we bounced over rocks and barely missed a tree.

Somehow Charles managed to stop the bus without turning it over. Inside all was chaos. People were struggling to their feet, screaming and crying. Orlando had dropped his gun and was trying to retrieve it, but the other passengers were crowding the aisles, sheltering us from him.

Dragging Amy after me, I scrambled through an open rear window. Ignoring a voice shouting *"Deténganse,"* we dropped to the ground.

"Run!" I screamed at Amy as we scrambled to our feet outside the bus. "Run!"

Keeping our heads down, we sprinted uphill toward the road, toward the Volkswagen, toward Grace and Phillip who were yelling, "Felix, Amy, hurry!"

"¡Deténganse!" Orlando roared from behind us as a bullet hit the earth ahead of me, kicking up a puff of dust.

"Stop!" Charles shouted. "Stop, you little beasts!"

Another bullet whined past my shoulder, but I didn't look back. I kept my head down and raced toward the Volkswagen's open door.

"Come on!" Phillip cried. "Come on!"

Then Phillip was grabbing at us, pulling us into the Volkswagen, and it was moving even before Amy had her feet inside. A bullet cracked a side window as Grace accelerated.

"Get down!" she yelled. "Stay on the floor!"

More bullets hit the Volkswagen, shattering the rear window, but Grace didn't even swerve. She drove like a stuntwoman in a movie, and in a few seconds we were out of range.

"Felix, Amy," she said, glancing over her shoulder. "You are all right?"

I took a quick look at myself. No bullet wounds, just the old gash on my leg, a few more scrapes and bruises on the rest of me, and lots of dirt. "I guess I'm okay," I said, hardly daring to believe it. "But how did you know we were on the bus?"

"We saw you sneak on before it left town," Phillip said, "but we couldn't do anything because Orlando and Charles came walking into the square right after you got into the bus. They just missed seeing us."

Grace nodded. "Now we must get back to Segovia." Turning the van sharply, she roared onto a highway as if Orlando and Charles were still chasing us.

Hanging on to a little loop over the window, Phillip shook his head. "Back home, she'd get a speeding ticket," he said, but you couldn't miss the admiration in his voice.

"Is your ankle okay?" Amy asked him.

Phillip winced a little and shrugged. "Grace says it's broken, but she splinted it the best she could." He extended his ankle, tightly wrapped in strips of torn cloth. "It still hurts," he said. "But I haven't cried once."

"How did Grace find you?" I asked.

"When Orlando came back and discovered we were gone, he was mad at first, then he and Charles got drunk," Phillip said. "Grace waited till they passed out, and then she took the Volkswagen and came looking for us. Señora Perez told her she thought we might be hiding in the hills near her farm.

"Thank goodness she didn't tell Orlando that," Amy said.

"Señora Perez was pretty much on our side by then," Phillip said. "In fact, if she'd seen us, she would've hidden us in her house."

Amy and I looked at each other. Like me, she was probably wishing she'd known that earlier. It would have saved us a lot of agony.

Phillip frowned at Amy and me. "You sure were hard to rescue," he said. "Once we thought we saw you, but you ran away. Then, after you got on the bus, we decided to go to Segovia and get the police, but Phillip and Orlando started chasing us. Wow, it was like being in a movie."

While Phillip acted out what had happened, complete with sound effects, I looked out the window at the people in the cars we were passing. I wondered what they'd say if they knew what had just happened to us.

"I hope Orlando doesn't hurt the other people on the bus," Amy said. "None of this was their fault."

"Except for that one old lady," I corrected her. "If she'd listened to us instead of thinking we were gypsies, we'd have gotten to the police station a long time ago."

Just then I noticed a bag on the seat beside Phillip. "Is that food?" He nodded.

Rummaging around, I grabbed a hunk of cheese and climbed up into the front seat beside Grace. "I was right about you all along," I told her through a mouthful of cheese. "You're a true citizen of the world, plus you're the best driver I ever saw."

Grace smiled at me, but her face was pale. One of her eyes was purple and swollen shut, and her upper lip was puffy.

"What happened?" I asked her.

"*Nada de nada,*" she said. "It is nothing. When Orlando came back, he blamed me for your escape. It is the way of a coward to beat up a woman."

She spat out the window to show her contempt for Orlando. "Now the bus is wrecked. Who will he blame for that?"

Looking at Grace closely, I realized her tee-shirt was wet. "You're bleeding," I gasped. "You've been shot."

"Do not worry," Grace said, "it is a mere flesh wound."

"But the blood."

"Just a trickle." She glanced at her arm and bit her lip.

"This kidnapping," she said, "what a great disaster it has been for me."

"The great Spanish kidnapping disaster," I said. "That's what it's been all right. The worst thing that ever happened to me."

"But almost over for you, Felix. Look." Grace pointed at a highway sign. "Five kilometers to Segovia. Very soon you will be safe again. But what of me? I will go to jail, I will be deported. Your disaster is done, but I think my disaster has just begun."

"What do you mean? You rescued us," I said.

"Yes, but before? When I told Charles and started all this. Will you tell that part?"

Amy and Phillip were leaning over my seat, watching Grace and listening. I looked at them and put my finger to my lips. Phillip nodded at once, but Amy hesitated.

"I don't want to seem ungrateful," Miss Perfect told Grace, "but you knew what was going to happen when you took us to the windmills."

"Ah, then I did not know of Orlando and how he would change things," Grace said. "That day in Segovia it seemed fair to get the money for the poor children from the rich American parents."

Grace frowned so fiercely I was worried she might decide to keep us for the ransom after all.

"But you could be dead at this very moment, and it would be my fault," she added. "I feel very bad to have trusted Charles, *muy estúpida.* Never did I intend any harm to befall you, you must believe me."

Grace struck her chest for emphasis and winced as if she had hurt herself.

"I think we should say they kidnapped *all* of us," Phillip said. "Including Grace."

I nodded and leaned toward Grace. "This is how we'll tell it," I told her. "You took us to see the windmills, and Charles and Orlando grabbed all four of us. You knew them, you told them we were visiting the windmills, but you had no idea they would *kidnap* us."

"The police will not believe this," Grace said sadly. "They will see the peepholes."

"Peepholes?" Phillip stared at Grace.

"Loopholes," I said, "she means loopholes."

Grace smiled. "I have so much trouble with the little funny things you say."

She turned off the road, and we saw Segovia on the hill above us, glowing golden in the afternoon sunlight just as it had three long days ago. As Amy bounced up and down with anticipation, I turned to her.

"There won't be any loopholes or peepholes if we all agree about what happened," I told her. "Are you going along with Phillip and me or not?"

Amy looked at Grace, at the blood drying on her arm, at her black eye and swollen lip. She frowned and thought hard.

"Come on, Amy." Phillip poked her in the side. "Say 'yes.' You have to. She saved our lives."

I leaned toward Amy. "You don't want Grace to go to jail, do you? Not after all she's done to make things right?"

Amy twirled a long strand of hair tightly around her finger. Narrowing her eyes, she stared at me. "If I say 'yes,' " she said to me, "will you promise never to say another word about my mother's music appreciation professor?"

Now it was my turn to think hard. As much as I hated to promise, I knew Grace was more important than silencing Amy with a telling blow like the music appreciation professor.

Reluctantly I said, "If I promise not to mention the professor, will you promise not to say mean things about my mother's cooking?"

Amy sighed. "I thought we were making a bargain about Grace. I don't see what your mother's cooking has to do with going to jail."

"It's a compromise," I said. "It won't kill you."

"Then maybe you should swear to stop acting like a know-it-all." Amy glared at me.

"And you could quit being such a goody-goody!" I was getting mad now.

"Girls, girls, what way is this to talk?" Grace stared at us. "Surely from this great disaster you have learned to be sisters."

Phillip squinted at us. "Grace is right," he said. "You're acting like barbarians. And, besides, the police station is straight ahead. We have to agree on our story before they start asking questions."

Amy and I looked where Phillip was pointing. Sure enough, at the end of the narrow street was a building with a sign over the door that said *Policía*.

"Oh, all right!" Amy slid down in her seat. "I'll go along with you, but if Grace gets away with it, she better not ever kidnap anybody else!"

Grace glanced at Amy. "Believe me, I will never do such an outrage again," she said. "I have learned my lesson."

Then the citizen of the world turned even paler and slumped over the steering wheel. Before I could figure out where the brake pedal was, the Volkswagen jumped the curb, climbed the steps like a windup toy, and came to a sudden stop halfway through the door of the police station.

19

Our sudden appearance at the police station caused quite an uproar. We were immediately surrounded by armed policemen, and for a moment I thought we were going to be shot on the spot as terrorists. Fortunately, someone realized we were too young to be dangerous and an even greater disaster was averted.

Despite his broken ankle, Phillip grabbed his phrase book out of my back pocket and added to the confusion by trying to explain who we were in Spanish. To my relief, one of the detectives spoke English and soon figured out we were the kidnapped children everyone was looking for.

"And this one?" he asked, meaning Grace who was still slumped over the steering wheel. If she hadn't moaned, I would have thought she was dead, she was so still and pale.

"She rescued us," Phillip and I said as an ambulance arrived.

Anxiously I watched the two men lift Grace out of the van and lower her gently to a stretcher. Except for her black eye, Grace's face was ashen against the red hair fanned out around it. Still caught in a tangle was the pink flower, its petals curled and rimmed with brown.

"Is she going to be all right?" I asked the doctor bending over her.

He nodded, and the detective said, "Take her to the hospital. The questions will be later."

Before the men rolled Grace away, she opened her eyes and smiled. "You see, Felix?" she whispered. "Did I not tell you this was a great disaster for me, the worst ever?"

The detective turned to us as the stretcher disappeared into the ambulance. "This woman is Grace, the stranger who took you to the windmills?"

"She was kidnapped too," I said.

"By Orlando and Charles," Phillip added quickly. "You better get them. They wrecked a bus in the mountains, and they have guns. They might hurt the passengers."

In response to this information, several police cars soon roared away. Then someone noticed Phillip's injured ankle, and, by the time Mom and Don arrived, we were drinking Cokes and feeling better than we had since we'd set out to see the windmills.

At the sight of me, her only child, safe and almost sound, Mom threw her arms around me and burst into tears. "Oh, Felix, Felix," she sobbed. "Are you sure you're all right? I was so scared. I was afraid I'd never see you again."

"You almost didn't," I said. My arms tightened around her and I cried too. Never had her hair smelled so nice to me. Never had her body felt so warm and comforting. "I thought I was going to get killed for sure."

"I can't believe I let you go off with that woman," Mom said. "How could I have been so irresponsible?"

"It wasn't Grace's fault." I stopped crying and drew back so I could see Mom's face. "Charles and Orlando followed her. They kidnapped all of us, Grace too."

"But she rescued us!" Phillip shouted. "She got shot, and they took her away in an ambulance."

Don turned to Amy. "Is Phillip right?" he asked as if he couldn't believe his own son.

There was a tiny silence. Phillip and I both held our breath and waited to see what Miss Perfect would say.

"If it hadn't been for Grace," Amy said, "we'd all be dead right now."

"Muerto!" Phillip yelled. "Bang! Bang! *Muerto!"*

After another flurry of hugging and kissing and crying, Don asked the detective if we could leave. "My son should have his ankle x-rayed, and Felix has a bad cut on her leg."

The detective leaned back in his chair and steepled his fingers on his chest. He scrutinized Phillip, Amy, and me, then leaned forward and smiled at us. "We will have to question these three again," he said to Don, "but I think they have suffered enough for now."

•

That night, Phillip, Amy, and I were in a lovely clean hotel room, bathed, fed, and rested. Phillip was sporting a big, white cast on his left leg and hopping around on one crutch. I was balancing myself on the other because my bandaged leg was still stiff and sore. Not wanting to be left out, Amy claimed she had a headache, and no one could prove she didn't.

From the Spanish evening news, we learned that Orlando and Charles were both in custody. By the time the police found the bus, the passengers had overcome our enemies and tied them to a tree. As the television camera moved in on Orlando and Charles, we could see the passengers in the background, laughing and talking. The baby had stopped crying, and even the old ladies were smiling. Charles and Orlando were the only bad sports in the group. They were obviously not enjoying themselves.

"What an awful man." Mom stared at a closeup of Orlando's face as Phillip attempted to translate the reporter's account of his criminal background.

I shivered and slid closer to her, glad for the security of her arm around me. Even though I knew he was now in jail, it scared me to see Orlando glaring into the camera lens, his cobra eyes still full of menace.

Charles's face appeared next, downcast, unhappy, ashamed.

"He graduated from Cambridge," Phillip translated, "and he's never done anything bad before this."

"I hope they throw the book at him," Don said.

Then it was Grace's turn. She was sitting in a hospital bed, and her bandaged arm, black eye, and split lip made her look the part of a victim.

According to Phillip, Orlando and Charles had told the police Grace was their accomplice. Although she admitted telling them, her old friends, about us, she denied any role in our kidnapping. The reporter pointed out that we backed up Grace's account. He seemed to think Orlando and Charles were lying.

After the news program, Mom hugged me. "I'm just so glad you're safe," she said. Then she burst into tears, something she'd been doing ever since she saw me in the police station.

"Oh, Felix," she said, "you don't know what Don and I have been through, sitting here in this hotel room, waiting for news, scared to death we'd never see you again."

"Yes," Don agreed, "we went to the embassy, the police, the press, and they all told us the same thing. There was nothing we could do but wait. They were doing all they could."

To my surprise, he put one arm around Amy and the other around me. Hugging us both, he said, "Well, it's all over now. Thanks to Grace, we have the three of you back, safe and happy."

From behind, Phillip slung his arms around Don's neck. Phillip's head was so close to mine, I could smell the shampoo he'd used, but for once I didn't feel like pushing him away. I didn't even want to pull away from Don. In fact, it was kind of nice sitting close to him. Maybe he'd turn out to be an all-right dad after all.

Then I thought of Grace, lying alone in the hospital. "What will happen when Grace gets well?" I asked. "Will she have to testify against Orlando and Charles?"

"I suppose so," Don said.

"How about us?" Phillip asked. "Will we have to be there too?"

Don slid an arm around Phillip. "I don't know yet," he said. "We'll talk to the police tomorrow. I imagine we have a lot to learn about Spanish law, something we sure didn't plan on when we left home."

I leaned against Mom, listening to Phillip and Don discuss legal matters. Once again, I was safe. I'd bathed and changed my clothes, Amy had done something to improve my hair, and I'd had a delicious dinner. For the first time, I felt like I was part of a real family.

But what about Grace's children? The starving ones she'd told me about? They weren't safe. They weren't comfortable. They hadn't had a delicious dinner. And they weren't going to get the money she had wanted them to have.

Straightening up, I looked at Mom. "Don't you think we should give Grace a reward for rescuing us?"

Mom stared at me. "Why, Felix," she said, "I never thought of that. Of course we should."

"And my father," I said, "could you ask him to contribute? He can afford it."

Mom turned to Dad. "What do you think?" she asked.

"Felix is right," he said. "We can certainly give Grace two or three thousand dollars, and Felix's dad can easily match that. Grace deserves something for endangering her life to save our children."

•

The next afternoon, Phillip, Amy, and I were allowed to visit Grace. When we entered her room, she was sitting up in bed reading a book, but she dropped it when she saw us.

"Children," she cried, "oh, what a happy surprise to see you again! And you are all right? No bad effects from our ordeal?"

While Phillip showed her his cast, I asked Grace about her injury. "It was nothing," she insisted. "No broken bones, just blood loss. I will be out of here in a couple of days, they say."

From the size of her bandage, I was pretty sure Grace was minimizing the bullet wound, but her color was better, and she looked almost as beautiful as she had the first day I'd seen her.

"This is for you." I set a huge floral arrangement down on the nightstand. "From our parents."

As Grace thanked me, I plucked one yellow flower from it and handed it to her. "For your hair," I said.

Grace took the flower but, with the use of only one arm, she couldn't put it in her hair. "Here, you do it, Felix, please."

I poked the stem gently into her hair, just above her ear. "There," I said.

Then I handed her an envelope. "This is for you too, from Mom and Don, from my father, and from Amy and Phillip's mother."

Without opening the envelope, Grace stared at me. "I do not understand," she said.

"It's a reward," Phillip butted in.

"For saving our lives," Amy added.

While we watched, Grace tore open the envelope and

took out the money. For a few seconds, she stared at it. "Oh," she said. "It is too much. I do not deserve it. Not after what I did. This is all my fault, Phillip's broken bone, your cuts and bruises, the fear and pain — I caused it all and your parents do this for me. If they knew, they would not give me anything."

With tears running down her cheeks, she thrust the envelope toward me. "Take this back, Felix. I will tell the truth, admit what I have done, go to jail as I should."

Gently I laid the envelope on her lap. "Please take it," I said. "It's partly my fault too. I told you so many lies in Toledo about how rich we were. If I hadn't made that stuff up, you might never have thought of kidnapping us."

Grace looked at the envelope again, at the money poking out of it. "For the children then," she said, and pressed the envelope to her chest. "I will take it for them, the starving ones."

"All of it?" Phillip asked. "Don't you want to keep some for yourself?"

"The children are the ones who need it, not me," Grace insisted. "It must go to them, every cent, to make up for what I did."

"But what will you do?" I asked her. "Where will you go?"

"There is still much of the world for me to see," Grace said. "I will journey onward, but I will be careful. No more disasters for me, Felix. I will watch out for the ones like Orlando and Charles, believe me."

As I perched on the bed beside her, Grace said, "Open the drawer, please, Felix, in the nightstand."

Obediently I slid it open. It was empty except for two gold hoops, my earrings, the very ones I'd thrown at Grace the day we'd been kidnapped.

"I saved them for you," Grace said, "just in case you might want them again."

I took them out and slowly fastened them in my ears. Grace and I smiled at each other. "They look nice," Grace said, "my little *gitana.* May they bring you luck always."

The room was quiet for a moment. Then Phillip sat down beside me and leaned toward Grace. "Come to America," he said suddenly, "and visit us. We have a big house."

"But no swimming pool and no Jacuzzi," I said. "No horse, either."

"There's a guest room, though," Amy added. "You could stay as long as you like."

I stared at her, too surprised to say anything, but Amy wasn't looking at me. She was smiling at Grace.

As Grace tried to hug all three of us, Mom and Don stepped into the room. While they thanked Grace for what she had done, I caught Amy's eye and winked at her. She smiled at me then, and I decided that having a sister might not be so bad after all. Especially if we could keep our promises to each other.

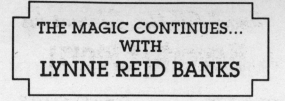